A ROUND HALF-DOZEN

SHORT STORIES

Best wishes,

Alamukanee

Kraftgriots

A ROUND HALF-DOZEN

SHORT STORIES

Adebayo Lamikanra

Published by

Kraft Books Limited
6A Polytechnic Road, Sango, Ibadan
Box 22084, University of Ibadan Post Office
Ibadan, Oyo State, Nigeria
Tel: 234 (2) 8106655
E-mail: kraftbooks@yahoo.com
krabooks@onebox.com

First published 2002

ISBN 978-039-063-4

=KRAFTGRIOTS=
(A literary imprint of Kraft Books Limited)

First printing, June 2002

Contents

Contents

Lucid Interlude

I had not set eyes on Ade for more than one year and I was not quite sure that he was much less robust than he was before. There had been rumours, vague as such rumours are wont to be, that he had been suffering from some kind of illness which, depending on your source, varied from the mysterious to the terminal. Maybe I had been mentally prepared for a sparer version of the man and was therefore not much disturbed by what I took to be the loss of a few pounds and inches from what, even in normal circumstances was an unremarkable frame.

'Ade, Ade!' I shouted when I saw him at the palm-wine bar just outside the university campus.

'My man, how are you, and where have you been all these days?' I gushed, my enthusiasm bubbling over like froth on the surface of a young and vigorous wine.

'Oh, I am fine' replied Ade, a little listlessly I thought, but definitely not anything as warm as my own greetings had been.

'Yes, I am fine now and getting better all the time, so I guess I have a great deal to be thankful for' he went on in his dead voice.

'What do you mean, getting better? Okay! I heard that you have been ill, but since nobody could supply any detail, or reliable information about your condition, I just refused to take it seriously.'

'Well, take it from me, I have suffered a great deal in the last fifteen months. I am surprised that you haven't noticed that I have lost a great deal of weight.'

'Losing weight is no longer an index of illness you know. True, you must weigh less than you used to but so have so many people that your weight loss does not mark you out in any special way.'

Ade laughed heartily at this point.

'Yes, you can say that my friend. The situation in this country is now so bad that many people in what can be regarded as the best of health are nevertheless shedding the plump look from enforced fasting', said Ade, his face still glowing with mirth as he took a long drink from the calabash in front of him.

'I am very sorry that you have been ill, but now that you have put all that behind you, I expect to see more of you around the campus' I replied in what I hoped were tones bulging with sympathy.

'I did not tell you that I had been ill', Ade shot out in a way that conveyed a strong impression of impatience.

'Yes, I have lost a great deal of weight' he continued in the same aggressive tone. 'I have lost weight, not from the ravages of any disease known to man, but from the attempt to treat a condition which existed only in the twisted imagination of the so-called doctor who claimed to be treating me.'

'I don't understand you' I replied a trifle hesitantly since I did not want to upset the man any more than I had done already.

'How can you be treated for a non-existent disease condition, and even more than that, how can the treatment be so drastic that you are now showing the scars of a terrible illness?' I wanted to know.

'All will be revealed, all will be revealed, my dear Watson' said Ade in the manner of Sherlock Holmes, as he got up from the table. 'All will be revealed', he repeated, 'as soon as I get back from paying my water rates. So fortify yourself with some more of this excellent palm-wine and await my return with impatience' he called over his shoulder as he walked away from our table, dragging his right leg after him, giving the impression that that foot was much heavier than the other.

'How can this man insist with such vehemence that he has not been, or indeed, not ill when he appears to be carrying a large burden of ill-health on his bowed shoulders?' I mused as I swallowed a thoughtful draught of palm-wine. It even crossed my mind that sitting with him in such a closed space may be dangerous to my health and I would have beaten a careful retreat from any further intercourse but for the fact that my curiosity about Ade begged, or rather, demanded immediate satisfaction. So I waited. Ade returned looking much more cheerful than before, which was something of a relief to me because I really did not know how I would respond to a discourse punctuated with tears and reeking with self-pity.

'It is really good to be here, breathing the sweet air of freedom' were Ade's first words on his return.

'Why are you talking about freedom, when as far as I can judge, you have not been in prison?'

'Prison is not the only institution where you lose your freedom' Ade snapped. Then he shook his head gently from side to side. 'I forget that you have not had cause to think about your freedom recently, if ever, so your naiveté can be forgiven' he continued in a much milder tone.

'Well. Take it from me, there are many places where you can lose your freedom more effectively than within the walls of a prison. I have been in one of these and I know just what I am talking about.'

I could see that the spark which had animated him only moments before was fading quite rapidly and I was afraid that he might lapse into stubborn silence and not tell his story. So, I tried to bring him right back to the present in the hope that he may thereby be encouraged to open the floodgates of his mind. But I need not have worried. Like the famous ancient mariner, he was in the grip of a powerful urge to unburden himself, and in doing so, find some peace.

Without any attempt at a preamble, Ade began his story.

'You know about my brother, I am sure.'

I nodded assent since like many people who were friendly with Ade, I knew about his brother's tragic death in a motor accident a couple of years before. Jare had been going to attend a friend's wedding in Benin when the bus in which he was travelling was halted by armed robbers who had stopped the bus by throwing a nail-studded plank in its path. The bus was travelling so fast however that the driver could not bring it to a halt. As he jammed a heavy right foot on the brake, the vehicle full of screaming passengers took off like a rocket, spun in the air like a toy under the control of an exuberant kid and was hurled down a steep slope into a ravine. There were only two battered survivors who told their sad story through torn and swollen lips at a Benin hospital where they had been taken by a couple of brave men. The poor victims had been brought out of the bus by some villagers on their way to the farm and laid by the side of the road for more than two hours before the brave men came along to take them to hospital. Other motorists who had passed that way before them, shook their heads in passive compassion, or crossed themselves fatalistically before speeding off to attend to less dangerous matters.

'My brother and I were close, very close and although I knew that he was dead, I just could not accept it. Besides, I kept hearing his voice. He was always talking to me, just as when he was alive,' Ade went on to inform me.

'Were you not scared of hearing your brother's voice from the grave?' I asked.

'No', he replied gently, 'and try not to ask so many questions as these are just interruptions.

'No, I was not scared at all' he continued. 'Indeed, it was a comfort. It was an assurance that what was between us was stronger than death and in a way, I was much comforted by this. We talked about everything except death and would have continued our indulgence in these conversations but for the fact that I grew rather careless and forgot that most people would have been alarmed had they come to know that I was in the habit of talking to a dead man. If you asked me at the time, I would have told you that all the conversations with my brother went on in my head, but that was not true. One day, Jare and I were deep in conversation about one of the girls he was going out with when I noticed my mother looking at me in frank astonishment and fear as she listened to my animated discussion apparently with a phantom.

' "Whom are you talking to?" she croaked when she noticed that I had, at last become aware of her presence.

'Like a fool, I promptly replied that I was telling my brother about Dupe, the girl he was going out with at the time of his death. I saw naked fear in her eyes and should have been warned, but I took no more notice of her than a total stranger did. I was too wrapped up in the world, which I had created for my brother and I to care about what anyone, least of all my mother would think about what must everywhere be regarded by everyone as being very strange. Completely overwhelmed by what I said the poor woman did an immediate about-turn and shuffled slowly out of the room.

'After this strange encounter, I noticed that my mother was always giving me strange looks, which suggested that she was thinking about me. But out of fear of what I might reveal, she refrained from asking me a direct question about my conversations with the dead and I did not volunteer any information either. The conversations continued and no doubt they were not in my head. They were distinctly audible to my mother who heard them with growing alarm.

'About two weeks after my mother first overheard my conversations with Jare, my father called me into his room, at a time when everybody else had retired to bed. I sat down rather gingerly in the chair he pointed to because I was not used to talking much with him and besides, I felt instinctively that he was going to talk about Jare.

' "Sit down Ade," said my father very quietly, almost in a whisper. . "Sit down and make yourself comfortable because this may take some time."

' "Thank you sir" I replied, trying to obey his injunction about making myself comfortable. Tried as I did however, I just could not manage it.

' "How are you?" he asked with concern, giving the impression that he was not expecting the stock answer of "fine", or whatever equivalent word I cared to use. He asked because he really did want to know exactly how I felt.

' "Things are rather difficult at this time sir" I replied truthfully.

' "Humph" was his immediate response. "I know you must be under a great strain right now, but you know, life must go on. Jare's time here is finished and we must all accept that and get on with the rest of our lives. Losing people close to us is part of life itself and we must not allow any particular loss to dim our eyes for too long, or else we will not be able to see and take chances which come our way. You see, such chances are few and far between and must be seized whenever they arise or, we may live to regret those missed chances."

'He probably wanted me to make a response to him, but what could I say? I suppose I was far too depressed to think of anything so I remained mute, my chin very close to my chest and my thoughts in my brother's grave.

' "From what your mother has told me..." I heard my father's voice from far away, farther away than Jare's grave, "you think far too much of your dead brother and I don't think that the way you are carrying on is healthy. Look I am his father you know, and love him as much as you do, but I haven't given myself up to morbid thoughts because that will not be fair to you and the others. Your mother, in the way of all mothers is shattered by Jare's death and you, more than anybody else must comfort her. But, as things stand, she has to comfort you and that is too difficult for her to do."

'I still could not utter a word, any word at all. I just sat there, cowering like a whipped cur.

' "In any event", continued my father, still as far away as ever, "what is this I hear about your holding conversations with a dead man?"

'My head jerked up as if on its own accord and for the first time, I thought that this was something I could talk about. Had I known what a dangerous topic it was, I would have avoided it like a thousand plagues. But, that is all with the benefit of hindsight. I seized what I thought was a golden opportunity to tell my father about my audio intercourse with my brother on the other side of the great divide.

' "It started even before Jare died", I began without any hesitation.   "We found over the years that we could "talk" to each other when we were far apart, but this happened rarely and we were hardly conscious of it. Looking back, I can now see that it was happening. For example, whenever he travelled, I always knew precisely when he would be back, sometimes without having been told that he had travelled. In any case, I knew that something was seriously wrong with him on the day he died, long before anyone told me about the accident. I woke up that day feeling very anxious about something, which I could not define. And I had no idea about what it could be until around the time that he must have died when I started to get the feeling that he was trying very hard to tell me something of vital importance. I carried the dreadful feeling of anxiety with me until the following day when you told me that Jare had died. The strange thing to me was that he was trying to console me, telling me not to be sad and things like that. Since then, he has been in constant touch with me and I am beginning to think that this is what is keeping me from going mad".

'At the word "mad", my father's head jerked up in a way, which suggested that it had a life of its own.

' "Mad? What do you mean by that?" he asked in considerable alarm. "What makes you think that you may go mad and how long have you harboured such thoughts?"

' "I know that I am not mad sir and I don't think that there is any chance that I am mad. It is just that there are times when I am in such black despair that I begin to fear that I could be driven insane by grief."

' "Look, my son, madness is not a thing to joke about and I am taking this grave revelation very seriously indeed. I know that you university people do not pay any attention to us when we talk about these things, but I have always been worried about the sanity of each and everyone of you because..."

'At this point, his voice dropped to a whisper so that there could be no chance of his being overheard by anybody.

' "Your uncle that lived in Kafanchan went mad and since this thing runs in families, we have to be very careful. You understand, don't you, that this is not something that you can go around telling people because it will do considerable damage to your prospects of getting married in the future."

'I did not believe for a moment that what happened to my uncle who was long dead anyway had anything to do with me. But my father's mien as he spoke to me was so grave that I knew that it was not the time for scoring cheap points of biology. I had to work very hard to prevent a smile from stealing across my countenance because his weighty revelation about my poor uncle was indeed a common item of intelligence within the extended family. I thought that at that time, everyone knew that before he died, my uncle was bouncing in and out of the asylum like an energetic rubber ball. Besides, my cousins, far from suffering any form of stigma that their father's condition could have inflicted on them, did not take any pains to conceal their father's madness from us. As far as they were concerned, it was just one of those things which could not be helped. I was however amazed that my father was blissfully unaware of the fact that a great many people knew that his brother was tapped in the head. I was not about to make him any wiser, so I kept my mouth shut.

'I had noticed long before this interview that my father did not have the capacity for confronting problems head on and preferred to work around them, sometimes by simply pretending that they did not exist at all. I confidently expected him to bring our uncomfortable discussion to a quick conclusion and was not disappointed. He advised me to go to bed, but to discourage my brother from keeping in touch with me, or else I might find myself in a load of trouble. Enough trouble to make my life truly miserable.

' "Thank you sir", I said brightly, relieved that my ordeal was over and that I could go off and be by myself (and Jare) once again.

Little did I know that my troubles had barely started and I was going to be very much wiser before I saw any light in my life again.

'Two days after the momentous interview with my father, my mother overheard me, apparently mumbling to myself. But as far as I was concerned, I was telling Jare about a local politician who had been caught with a few kilograms of heroin in his very smart, custom-made briefcase on his arrival at the JFK Airport in New York, on a flight from Lagos. The case was thoroughly talked about by us and as usual, I was so engrossed in it that I did not notice that my mother was in a position to overhear practically every word of this apparent monologue. There can be no doubt that she reported this incident to my father who in turn passed the information on to his own mother.'

At this point, Ade looked up very sharply as if to check the level of my attention to his tale which as far as I was concerned, was not just strange but getting stranger by the minute. There was no way that my attention could waver in the circumstance in which I found myself, and Ade was evidently pleased that I was paying him the compliment of giving him my absolutely undivided attention. He was so pleased that he gave me a tight little smile and pointed to the full calabash in front of me, no doubt inviting me to take a drink. I duly obliged and, as he was thirsty from all that talking, he also took a long drink.

'Aha, that's better' he sighed as he wiped the foam from his lips with the back of his hand.

'Do you still have a grandmother?' he asked, rather irrelevantly, I thought.

'No. Unfortunately, both of my parents lost their mothers rather early in life and so I have no idea of what it means to have a grandmother' I replied nevertheless.

'If my experience with my grandmother is anything to go by, you have not missed a thing, my friend', was his surprising response.

'Both my grandmothers are still alive, very much alive and kicking. My paternal grandmother is threatening to live forever, at least as far as I can judge. She must be close to, or over ninety years old, but is still as sprightly as a woman roughly half her age. She guards all of us, and by all of us, I mean her eight surviving children, her four or five dozen grandchildren and a whole army of great-grandchildren with impressive alertness. She even has a few great-great-grandchildren and rules her clan with an iron hand. She is supposed to be a Christian, but the word, 'nominal' was invented specially for her. You see, she goes to church regularly all right, but she has not lost touch with the ancestors. No decision is taken within the family until she has consulted the household gods and a couple of fetish priests retained for just that purpose. When Jare died, she not only consulted her own priests but consulted several famous priests in an attempt to find out if anyone was responsible for his death. I don't know whether she found the answer to that riddle, but you can be sure that if she did not, it was not for want of trying.

'In any case, let us concentrate on what happened to me. As soon as my case was reported to my grandmother, she took complete charge and ordered my father to bring me home to her immediately. And of course, that order had to be obeyed no less immediately than she wanted it to be. Two days after the summons were delivered, I was taken to see my grandmother by my father who, as the distance between him and home diminished, appeared to shed his years. By the time he was lying prostrate in greeting before his mother, he conveyed the distinct impression that he was barely into his adolescent years.

' "Welcome, Ade", she crowed as soon as she saw me.

'She then launched into a lengthy and moving recital of my praise names, all of which suggested great prowess in what I am forced to admit, are imaginary battles. This notwithstanding, I rather liked the play on words, the most prominent feature of the recital.

'As soon as the ceremonials associated with welcome were completed, my grandmother and her son moved into conference, leaving me to my rather limited devices. All my cousins with whom I was familiar had flown the coop, leaving a few ancient relics with whom I had nothing in common, never mind that we were all closely related. It made me wonder what all the fuss about the thickness of blood was in aid of. I soon found that all I could do to keep me amused was to read a few scraps of newspapers which had long been used to wrap various items of cooked food.

'My father and his mother had been huddled together for nearly two hours before they called me over. One look at the old lady and I could not only see fear, but could smell it as well. Her fear was that my brother was trying to entice me over to the other side and she wanted to know if he had been giving me any instructions.

' "Has he asked you to do anything, anything at all?" she asked in a fierce whisper.

' "No, nothing", I answered without hesitation because that was the truth.

' "Whatever be the case" she said turning to my father, "I am still strongly convinced that we cannot afford to take any chances. We will go and see Baba Kobomoje first thing tomorrow morning and should know by midday what we have to do next."

'Baba Kobomoje lives and practises medicine in the traditional mode in a village some thirty kilometres away from our hometown. The last ten kilometres to his clinic, if you can call it that, is a crumbling road through cocoa farms and since not many people want to expose their vehicles to the unwisdom of travelling on that road, the clinic is virtually inaccessible. In spite of this obvious handicap to trade, or if you insist, practice, the clinic was crowded out with anxious clients which meant that we had to wait for more than three hours before we were ushered into the presence of the great man by a suitable obsequious aide.

'Ours was not a hurried consultation. Indeed the most impressive thing about the whole encounter was the man's massive patience. He listened impassively, his face a mask of immobility as first, my grandmother and then my father laid the case before him. They all ignored me. I might have not been there at all, so I tried to travel away from that room on the wings of my own imagination. Having discovered that there was absolutely nothing in that room to excite my interest, I took refuge in my own thoughts. In the room which was entirely bare of any furniture, all of us were sitting on mats and Baba Kobomoje was evidently listening very hard to what he was being told.

'The telling took a long time and at the end of it, Baba was nodding very wisely.

' "This is a simple and straightforward case", was his verdict.

'I must confess that I was very much relieved when I heard this because, although I was quite sure that there was nothing the matter with me, the attention which my elders were giving to this matter had begun to worry me more than a little bit.

' "Yes, this is a clear case, all the same, a case for Ebiyemiju in Odo Ifobi", he continued in a firm voice.

'Neither Ebiyemiju nor Odo Ifobi meant anything to me and what crossed my mind was that we were in for another cross-country trek. I was about to get up preparatory to making a departure from Baba's consulting room when I looked up to see a look of dismay on my grandmother's face. Why is she worried? I wondered, but then, sensing that I was looking at her, she recomposed her features very quickly and I could no longer be sure of what I had seen.

' "You may be wondering how I came to this conclusion so quickly. Well, there is really nothing to explain. I have seen several cases of this nature and I know enough about it to advise you to go off to Ebiyemiju immediately. Any delay will only make matters worse and you certainly cannot afford to have this happen."

'It was late in the day when we entered Odo Ifobi in an extremely wretched pick-up van fitted with long planks which served as seats of some sort. Most of the other passengers were on their way back from their farms and carried a terrific amount of luggage although it is difficult to include a couple of lively goats in this category. Those two animals, undeterred by the presence, the overbearing presence one might say, of so many human beings were as lively as only goats can be, and in that enclosed space, their antics were sheer murder.

'Odo Ifobi turned out to be no more than a few houses on either side of the miserable road which ran through it and beyond to several other settlements just about as clapped out as Odo Ifobi if not more so. As soon as we got out of the pick-up, my grandmother, sparkling as usual, arrested a passing urchin and ordered him to take us post-haste to Ebiyemiju's house. The little fellow promptly obliged in an enthusiastic manner, which could not ever have been contemplated by his more sophisticated urban counterparts.

'We should not have worried about finding our way to Ebiyemiju's house because, as we soon found out, his sprawling compound was the most, if not the only notable institution in the village. All other buildings were indeed described in relation to Ebiyemiju's house which in reality was a cluster of houses all roofed over with galvanised iron sheets. The roofs had become rust coloured from the effects of many cycles of the seasons, which had shown no mercy to man, nor beast or inanimate object.

'Although it was getting dark outside, the best word with which to describe the interior of the main building into which we were led was "gloomy". It was apparent that this was a building into which natural light was meticulously prevented from shining. As I was to find out, Ebiyemiju had a grouse against sunlight and took great pains to ensure that it did not touch any of his belongings within the protection of his roofs.

'We were led into a room, which was filled with all sorts of crudely carved chairs, but at first, we could not make out anything in the surrounding gloom. After a few minutes, we began to identify the contents of the room and were startled to find out that there were some people there apparently in a stupor and slumped in some of the chairs. None of them stirred and we were at a loss as to how to attract their attention long enough to inquire after the man of the house. We were on the verge of going out again when a large man, sporting a truly impressive belly walked briskly into the room and greeted us most cordially. Thus, I came face to face with my nemesis.

'The man who greeted us so cordially was Ebiyemiju himself. It was not possible in that half-light to make out any of his features, but the poor light could not prevent us from appreciating the muscular build of the man. He was a shade over six feet tall and although he had that great belly on him, there appeared to be very little fat to his bulk. He moved easily and quickly, giving the impression of being frequently, if not always on the move. Indeed, in a way, he was always on the move, or at least, part of him was. He was never without a white horsetail whisk, which he moved continuously to and fro, even in the middle of the most solemn conversation. For such a big man, he spoke in hushed tones and never raised his voice, probably because he had such a massive physical presence that he really did not need any vocal complementation to arrest attention.

' "Thank you my son", the old lady responded. "I trust that you and yours are well."

' "We thank God for everything, but above all, for good health without which nothing good can be accomplished. I welcome you to my home and hope that whatever it is that you have come looking for, you will find here."

' "We have come about this son of mine", she said, pointing to me.   "It seems that he is in the hands of evildoers, people who do not want to see other people making progress. It is a little over two months since we buried his elder brother and now this one says that his dead brother talks to him. His mother has heard him several times talking to himself but on being questioned, claimed that he was talking to his brother on the other side. Help me. Please help me. Save us from the calamity so that we are not made to suffer the jests of our enemies."

'No sooner had she finished making this passionate plea than she burst into tears and rent the air with sobs which seemed to have travelled up into her ancient throat right from the soles of her feet.

'My first response to this outburst of passion was surprise. Up till that point in time, I had not taken the situation seriously. It could even be said that I had up till then been faintly amused by it all. Those sobs brought me back to earth with a terrific bump as I found myself drowning in a sea of apprehension. I looked from my grandmother to my father who looked on with a bemused air. He looked like a man confronted by something far bigger than he was and there was no way that I could draw any encouragement from his perplexed countenance. The only person who looked to be in control was Ebiyemiju. He looked like somebody who not only had all the answers, but also had them at his fingertips. Ironically, it was this man who had my immediate confidence and his words suggested to me that this confidence was not misplaced. To be sure, he took his time over making his response but when it came I felt that he had spent his time usefully.

' "Ah, my mother, there is no need to cry. This is a problem only for those who have no experience of things like this. So the young man says he can speak with his dead brother. That is a minor problem. I have come across some people who claim to be in regular contact with an army of dead people. Now if you came and told me that he did nothing but hold conversations with his dead brother, I would have been worried. But the young man appears to lead a normal life and it is only now and then that he suffers from these delusions, so don't let us see beyond what we have in front of us."

'Although I was the subject of this discussion, there was no way I could make any contribution and so I held my peace even though I was very far from being at peace. My mind was seething with a cocktail of emotions with frustration beating annoyance into second place by a short head. Why? I wondered, are these people talking about me without even bothering to acknowledge my presence? I would have told them, if only they had bothered to ask me, that I was quite well in every respect, but they didn't. So I just sat there hoping that they would soon come to a decision that I could live with. Well, they did come to a decision, but it was not one that anyone should have been made to live with.

'Although Ebiyemiju thought that the case before him was a simple one, he nevertheless announced the decision that I should be allowed to remain with him for three months. This was to give him the opportunity to work on me so that he could defeat the evil people who were trying very hard to take full possession of my body in order to make me their slave. That anybody was trying to enslave me in any way was certainly news to me, but what really alarmed me was the impracticality of staying in Odo Ifobi whilst the university was in session. I felt that I had to make this point and I did.

'Ebiyemiju slowly turned his head in my direction and the look of surprise on his face could not have been more pronounced had he been a cat which had suddenly acquired the capacity for human speech.

' "Oh my God!" he rumbled. "We are talking about saving him from a terrible situation and he is talking about university lectures! What do you want with lectures if all you will be left with for a body, is an empty shell? You are only lucky that your parents and grandmother know enough about the ways of the world and brought you here for treatment. Better stop thinking about the university, or else, your case may quickly deteriorate and become hopeless."

' "Pay him no attention", my grandmother chipped in, her voice dripping with scorn. "What does he know about anything?" she wanted to know. "Look", she said, turning to me, "you may have read all the books in the world, but when it comes to things like this, you are a nobody. But for what your parents and I have been doing on your behalf, you would not have been in the university or even in the world. You are like a corpse, which cannot appreciate anything done on its behalf, so just keep your mouth shut. Only goodness knows what you have done to bring this trouble down on your own head. In spite of our efforts, you are now going around talking to yourself like a madman. Don't let me hear you say anything about the university again. At least not until you are back to normal."

'I turned to my father as if for support, but the look of utter bewilderment on his face suggested that I would not find succour from that source. It was plain to see that the poor man was in the grip of something more powerful than he was. More than that however, he gave me the impression that I was from that time on very much on my own and that he was prepared to accept whatever was going to develop from the situation.

'By this time, it had become quite dark and lamps had been lit. Our host, gracious as anyone could be expected to be, offered us a rich supper which in spite of my mounting apprehension, I ate heartily. After all, I had not had the opportunity of any meal that day and being in good physical shape, my body, thoughtless as only a young body can be, demanded instant and extensive nourishment and I was happy to be in a position to oblige it.'

At this point in Ade's fascinating narration, my own bodily needs forced themselves into my consciousness, no doubt because food had just been mentioned. We had been sitting in our little corner for a long time, but the story, both in its telling and its listening had blocked out every other thing and I was surprised to find that lights had been put on sometime before. All the people now sharing our temporary accommodation had come in since Ade started his story.

Once I became aware of my body's demand for food, I knew that the best thing to do was to get us something to eat so that we would not be disturbed thereafter. I therefore called over one of the waiters and ordered two plates of fresh fish pepper-soup and more palm-wine with which to lubricate the throats down which the soup was going to slide. Ade was also quite hungry because when the soup came, he drank it up very quickly, and having taken a generous swig of his wine, was ready to continue with his story.

'After supper was eaten, I began to wonder what manner of place we were in. All kinds of weird sounds were getting through to us from several parts of the compound and every now and then, a scream pierced the curtain of darkness around us and made my blood run cold. I wanted to ask questions about this, but my father and grandmother, completely exhausted by our exertions during the day were soon asleep in their chairs and I could not summon up the courage necessary to interview our host. In any case, I was on the edge of sleep myself so I did not have the necessary mental energy to think deeply about the situation.

'I had made myself comfortable in my chair and was trying to settle down to sleep when I was rapped on the head with a stick. I was awake in an instant and got up ready to defend myself when I saw that the rapper was Ebiyemiju who was offering me a drink. I took the proffered cup and put it to my lips but was discouraged from drinking it off by the pungent odour, which enveloped me as soon as the cup was brought under my nose. I looked up interrogatively at the man over the rim of the cup, but all he did was motion me to drink up. I refused.

' "Drink it up" Ebiyemiju pleaded. "It is very good medicine for the brain. It is sure to calm you down so that you will sleep better than you have ever done before."

'I put the cup back to my lips and took the first tentative sip. The main ingredient of the preparation was alcohol, fiery alcohol which brought tears to my eyes, but which turned out to be a pleasant vehicle for whatever drug it was carrying within it. I drank up and from then on remembered absolutely nothing.

'I woke up later, very much later in a room without any light, natural or artificial. Don't ask me for how long I was asleep, or more appropriately, was in a coma because even now, I do not have the faintest idea about how long I was *non-corpus mentis*. I woke up feeling very light in the head and ravenously hungry. I moved my head around me and for a minute thought that I had gone blind, so thick was the darkness in the room. I then tried to get up and found that my right foot was carrying a heavy weight which on tactile investigation, I discovered was a fat log of wood. I had been stripped down to my underclothes and it flashed through my mind, confused, as it was that I was a prisoner of some sort. The first emotion that went through me was fear. I had never been so thoroughly frightened in all my life. My heart was leaping about in my chest as if a hard taskmaster was whipping it. And there was a furious ringing in my ears as if all the bells in the world were being rung at the same time right inside my aching head. I tried to get up again but was so weak that I could not manage to do so. It was then that I started to shout like a man possessed. At first, I did not realise that I was making any sound, but I soon discovered that my vocal chords were still fully functional. I really let it rip and made more noise than was required to wake the dead. I kept up the volume of noise for a long time and was pouring with sweat before it dawned on me that I could not expect help from any quarters. I was completely on my own, with nothing to suggest that there was life outside that shuttered tomb. I shouted myself painfully hoarse and then stretched out on the floor for some well-deserved rest.

'I had been lying down in semi-stupor for another couple of hours or so before the door of what I was sure was a cell swung open to admit three men. One of them was carrying a lamp, the other an earthenware plate with some scraps of food. The other one was Ebiyemiju wearing a leather apron studded with cowries. He also held a shiny ram's horn in his left hand. The other two men hung back from me as if I was an unpredictably dangerous animal. Ebiyemijù however walked up boldly to me, squatted and put his hand under my chin and tilted my head up in order to see my eyes. I was at that time sitting on the floor in anticipation of some form of human contact. Without acknowledging my humanity however, Ebiyemiju turned to his assistants and began talking about me, almost as if I wasn't there.

' "This one is from the university. You know how those people read fat books, but have no sense. Nobody knows whom this puppy has offended, but he is clearly on the wrong side of somebody who is as wicked as he is powerful. His case is a pathetic one and if care is not taken, he would soon get out of control, roaming the streets as naked as the day he was born. He is so ignorant about the danger he is in that all he worries about is getting back to his studies, studies which were sure to contribute to his madness. He appears to be quite normal now, but as I have told you over and over again, this is only a calm before the storm. We must all watch him very carefully because he is possessed by spirits, which are not only evil but are also very cunning. They are still in the process of settling down in him so they are not ready to fully reveal their presence, but never fear, they will soon be tired of their game of hide and seek and then, heavens help him. The only hope for him is for us to be continuously vigilant and not take any chances whatsoever."

'As you can imagine, I listened to this nonsense with rising disbelief. I thought that the man had gone stark, raving mad and unfortunately, told him so. That stopped him in full flow, but if I thought that I had won a victory of any kind, I was soon made to see the error of my ways. In my carelessness, I did not notice that the crazy man had a whip in his right hand, which was in shadow. The words had barely left my mouth before the lunatic attacked me and thrashed the living daylights out of me. At the start of this assault, I was numb with surprise. After three or four strokes however, the pain, searing in its intensity broke through my numbness and caused me to writhe like a snake. But there was no escape from the blows, which rained down on me like hail in a storm. I screamed with pain and let loose a string of invectives against my tormentor who nevertheless kept up the punishment. Just as I thought that the beast was intent on beating me to death, the blows stopped as suddenly as they began. It was when I stopped shouting and heard Ebiyemiju's laborious breathing that I knew that he stopped the thrashing only because he sensed that further exertion was likely to have an undesirable effect on his own health. I knew there and then that my very life was in serious danger from this fiend and what more, I had no idea as to what to do to prevent him from terminating it whenever he wanted to do so.

' "As you can see, this case is worse than I thought. He has gone past the early stages of madness and is now in the very dangerous state of delusion. Notice how he was calling me a madman at the top of his voice. If we could question him closely, he would no doubt tell us that he is sane even though he is riddled through and through with the seeds of madness. His body is now home to some virulent evil spirits and it is our duty to get them out of him. As I have told you many times before, such spirits are only at home in comfortable quarters. Just look at him. He is clean, well-fed and very healthy. As long as he remains so, the offending spirits will only get more robust and dangerous. We have to make their habitat inhospitable by frequent beatings, very hard work and starvation. I must warn you however that you have to be very careful and make sure that the demons do not find you an attractive hiding place when we have succeeded in making life within our young friend unbearable for them. You must never be without protective charms whenever you are in his presence and neither of you must ever be alone with him in an enclosed space like this room."

'All throughout this lecture, the acolytes remained resolutely mute. They however looked like they were alert to any type of a danger with which they may be confronted and had the situation not been so grim, I would have found the whole thing rather amusing. As things were however, I knew that I could not indulge in such luxury, as it was likely to prove far too expensive in terms of blood and tears so I held my peace. It was at this point that I was finally fed.

'Under normal circumstances, I would not have given the food offered a second glance. As I said before, all I was given to eat could be described as scraps, odds and ends of what I hesitate to call food. Nevertheless, I attacked those scraps with impressive enthusiasm. I was only a little less hungry at the end of the meal than before, but I felt better for having eaten.

'Up till that time, I had not really tried to take stock of my situation, but now that I was conscious and locked up with all the time on my hands, I just had to make some sense of this nightmare. I turned my mind off my discouraging immediate environment and turned it inwards trying to sort things out within myself. But I soon found that I just could not concentrate. I was too distracted by fear and then physical demands, hunger, discomfort and calls of nature, which I could not ignore any longer. To make things unbearable, I was attacked by all sorts of biting insects, which appeared to have been sent from hell with specific instructions to inflict tortures on my person.

'I was still groping about in mental darkness when the mammoth scale of my predicament suddenly flashed through my mind like a bolt of lightning, illuminating my mind and at the same time, sending shafts of fear down my spine. There I was, as healthy mentally and physically as I could ever hope to be, locked up in an asylum presided over by a man who, as far as I could judge, was at least a trifle touched in the head, if not actively mad himself. It was clear to me that I was in considerable danger, if not from the "doctor", from the inmates, many of who must be insane. I was at this point in my meditation when a blood-curdling yell penetrated the obviously thick walls of my cell and blasted my eardrums as if to reinforce the reasons for my fears. I had always thought that thinking would solve any problem, or at least point the way to a solution. Well, I now appreciate that there was a limit to what can be achieved by thinking, as several hours of thought, which I had expended on this problem, did not seem to have yielded any fruits.

'I was in solitary confinement in that room for several days, how many I could not tell as I had no means of measuring the passage of time. It was always night in the room and so I was completely disorientated. I was hungry all the time as I was fed on very little food at distressingly infrequent intervals. If neglect could cure maladies, I would have been cured even to Ebiyemiju's satisfaction within a short period of time.

'My real introduction to Ebiyemiju's establishment occurred after several miserable days. Early one morning three hefty men came into my room, checked that my right foot was securely chained to the attached log of wood and then let me out into the courtyard. I was weak and the log was heavy, very heavy, so my progress was painfully slow in spite of the blows, which were rained on my bare back to encourage speed. When I finally emerged into the pale sunlight of the courtyard, I was amazed to see about sixty human beings in various stages of physical degeneration. Each of them attached to logs, which appeared to have been cut from the same tree, which furnished the encumbrance to which my right foot had been wedded. I was further surprised that they were all sitting quietly, like puppets before a performance. I had never experienced such silence from a group of people. It was as if they had all been drugged. Well, they were. All the patients were routinely drugged especially if they were not going to the farm on any particular day. I have never been interested in drugs and such other preparations, but I had not spent many weeks in Ebiyemiju's asylum before I noticed that a gnarled snake-like root was always being pounded in a mortar by one of Ebiyemiju's several wives. The powder obtained from this exercise formed the basis of the concoction with which we were all liberally dosed. It kept us as quiet as little mice, I can tell you.

'Look around you and you see people who are not satisfied with their lot in life. People who can just afford to eat three square meals everyday are unhappy because they cannot afford to eat more and better, whereas, those who can only manage two meals wish with all their heart that they could get three meals into their bellies each and everyday. Moving from a place of misery to one of less misery is, as I found that day, pure joy. In the period of my unilluminated solitary confinement, I was thoroughly miserable, so miserable that I thought that the end of the world, at least for me, was only around the corner. Being allowed to catch a glimpse of the sky was such a great improvement that my heart gave a leap as I was let out to look once more on the sky. I was able, once more to face my fellow human beings, never mind that they appeared to be about as lively as the logs to which they were chained.

'I had not been drugged that morning and had my wits about me. I was therefore at liberty to take a good and meaningful look at my fellow-sufferers. Being a famous healer, Ebiyemiju's establishment was full to overflow with supposedly mad people of every age and description. Some were very young, in their early teens and others were old, white-haired and stooped with age. There were about as many women as men. Some of the women were there with their children and a few of them were pregnant, one of them, very heavily so. I guessed quite rightly as it turned out that the ladies acquired their pregnancy right there in Ebiyemiju's establishment, which I thought showed the iron resilience of nature. I was rather disappointed later on to learn that the ladies had no say in the matter of becoming pregnant. There is the belief in these parts that making love to a madwoman brought good luck and there are many men looking to improve their luck and ready to pay for it. Many of such men paid cold cash to Ebiyemiju for the opportunity of indulging in this fancy. Apart from being an asylum, Ebiyemiju's place was a bordello of sorts.

'My coming out marked a turning point in my stay in Ebiyemiju's asylum. At least from then on, I had the opportunity of contact with other people. I was resolutely convinced that I was not mad, but that conviction was more than a little shaken when I discovered that not one of my fellow inmates admitted to being mad. Some of them were convinced without a shadow of doubt that not only were they sane, but that the rest of us were raving lunatics. My main problem was how I could convince anyone that I was not mad when others who were obviously stark raving mad were no less convinced that they were not touched by insanity. It did not take me very long to realise that the more I protested my sanity, the greater was Ebiyemiju's insistence that I was mad. At one time, remembering what someone told me a long time before, I thought I could get Ebiyemiju to think that I was well on my way to getting cured by admitting that I was indeed mad. Ebiyemiju was not fooled. The sly look, which he bestowed on me, told me plainly that he was on to me. "You sly dog" he seemed to say, "you are mad, quite mad and I know just what I am going to do to you." So, that attempt failed and life went on pretty much as before.

'Life going on pretty much as before does not mean that hole was anywhere near being pretty. On the contrary, life there was nothing if not grim, very grim indeed. Ebiyemiju promised to scare the evil spirits out of me. I don't know about evil spirits, but I can tell you that he scared me half to death, if not more. A man who eats three times a day just cannot appreciate how much less he actually needs to stay alive and even thrive. At Ebiyemiju's we all lived in that hazy boundary between starvation and survival. We were fed only once a day and that with a few odds and ends of all kinds of food, which had cheapness as their only common property. It did not matter what the symptoms of our varying conditions were, we were all subjected to the same treatment regimen, one of the most prominent factors of which was starvation. The quantity of food on offer was far from impressive and so there were no leftovers. Everything was wolfed down almost in the twinkling of an eye and we were only a little less hungry at the end of our meal than we were before.

'Ebiyemiju took money from our relatives for the privilege of ill-treating us. It is true however that some of the inmates had been there for so long that their long-suffering sponsors had abandoned them. It did not matter however to which category any of us belonged, we all laboured like slaves on Ebiyemiju's farms. We were taken in turns to do our share of weeding, digging and harvesting on one of Ebiyemiju's several farms. And how we were worked! From sun-up to sundown we were working almost non-stop, adding to our healer's obvious wealth by tilling his toil. It was at this time that the phrase, "sweat of your brow" began to mean something to me. I sweated, as I never did before. Ebiyemiju wrung all the labour that he could get out of each and everyone of us by setting some fiendish guards over us. It was they who saw to it that we were always working and that we did the work well. They had the authority to beat us as much as they thought was necessary and not once did they shirk their responsibility in this regard. They thrashed us with a will and they must have enjoyed doing so. Our misery was more than doubled by the fact that in spite of the demands made on our energy, we were not much better fed than when we were not working. Yes, there were times when we were not working, but it was necessity rather than any goodness of heart that made those times of respite possible. Ebiyemiju did not want any of us to drop dead on him because we were far more valuable alive than dead. Dead men can neither tell tales nor till the soil and since nobody cared about whatever tales we wanted to tell, keeping us alive to till the soil was a far more profitable option.

'Being under Ebiyemiju's unloving care opened my eyes to so many things that I think I have gained more from my seven-month stint with him than I can wring out of seven years in the university. But, talking about the university, it is surprising that being an undergraduate marked me out even in that place and many of my fellow sufferers thought that it was a mark of distinction to be associated with me. They all thought that my head had been turned by too much learning and it was funny to me to see confirmed lunatics demonstrating pity for me in their lucid moments. To them, my case was a tragedy and I was cast in the role of a pawn in a terrible game being played by the "wicked of the world". There were a few other people who were put in my category; the most prominent of these being a middle-aged man who had been brought home a few years before from Germany.

'Bode (not his real name) was not in the first flush of youth when he got a scholarship to study Engineering in what was then East Germany. He had been trying for years to go abroad to study and he had indeed lost all hope of success when the offer from Berlin came out of the blues. It was at the height of the cold war and there was a need for some balancing so that the East Germans were keen to show off their own Africans to the West Germans who already had Africans of their own. Bode's son was about six months old at the time but the poor man had no choice but to go out and seek all those academic qualifications which he yearned to have. Europe, viewed from a dingy, one-room apartment in a Lagos slum is a pretty alluring place and when going there also holds out the prospects for an engineering degree, Bode could hardly wait to get there. Unfortunately, what he saw at the other end was a far cry from what he had hoped to see.

'In spite of extensive propaganda, East Germany had very little if anything to offer. Accommodation was poor, nearly as bad as what Bode was used to back home. The weather was unkind especially Bode's first winter, which unfortunately broke all records for coldness. The situation might have been tolerable for the poor man if the natives had been friendly. But they were not. Most of those with whom Bode came in contact were actually quite hostile. They looked upon him as they would have looked at a dangerous and exotic parasite and treated him as such.

'Bode bore all these hardships with some equanimity. After all, he had come to get an engineering degree and all the suffering would be cancelled out by success in this regard. He therefore devoted all his time to his studies in the expectation that he would do well. His hopes did not materialise. First, he had to learn German. Unfortunately, he, for some inexplicable reason could not for the life of him make anything of the gibberish which was spoken by all the people with whom he came in contact. Long after his sojourn in Germany began, he was still trying to come to terms with the language. This being so, more than two years had gone by before he was declared proficient enough to proceed to the engineering course which brought him so far from home in the first place.

'Bode's performance in engineering was only a shade better than the disaster which language school was. Most things about the subjects he had to take were "Greek" to him. He kept failing his examinations and with each failure he sank deeper and deeper into black despair. Had he had the benefit of sympathetic company, he probably would have been able to keep going somehow. But he was all alone. His wife had refused to uproot herself from Lagos and as the years rolled by the link between them had become increasingly tenuous until it ceased all together.

'Bode was like a bomb waiting to explode and explode he did. In responding to a trivial racial insult, he unleashed such violence on his tormentor that the poor fellow was landed in hospital and Bode in police custody. There, it took six burly policemen to subdue him, but only temporarily. The man was clearly off his head and had to be transferred to an asylum from where he was deported back to Nigeria. His family, which had all but forgotten him completely, did not know how to cope with their strange relative and when he began to terrorise the neighbourhood, they had no choice but to bundle him off to Ebiyemiju's famous establishment. Thereafter, he was conveniently forgotten and by the time I became an inmate of that hellhole, he had become a permanent fixture of the place. True Bode behaved in a way that you would expect from a madman but for quite long periods he appeared to be as sane as anyone can hope to be. I had long and interesting discussions with him and it was as a result of these conversations that I was able to piece his story together.

'Bode and I because of our scholastic background were in high demand. Ebiyemiju loved to show me off as an example of people whose heads had been turned by books.

' "Look at this one", he was fond of saying pointing to me, or patting me on the head as if I was a faithful dog. "This one is a university undergraduate who has bitten off more than he can chew. He came here looking robust, rude with crude physical well-being and full up to the eye brows with the most potent of evil spirits. He is more dangerous than a snake because should one of those spirits ever get it into its head to find new quarters, nobody is safe. The irony of this situation is that the only ones safe from him are those who are already mad. Anyway, you have nothing to fear as long as you are with me. I have them under control even though I have not yet managed to flush them out of him. I will soon be trying a new and very powerful potion on him. Indeed, I am only waiting for the right time to give him this drug. After that, I will be very surprised if those spirits are still where they are now."

'Almost invariably, the visitors, who had great confidence in Ebiyemiju's powers, believed every word of this nonsense.

' "May God give you the strength to conquer", some of them prayed.

' "Amen", the response bubbled out of the great man as his visitors moved on to be presented with another interesting case. Bode, because he had gone all the way to Germany and besides, was sometimes violent, was a bigger attraction than I ever could be and got more oohs and aahs out of the visitors.

'In that asylum, there was no way for me to mark the passage of time. I was not expecting to be released after a certain time and there was indeed no guarantee that I would ever be released. For a long time after I got there, nobody was discharged, but for two wretches who died, both of them in inexplicable circumstances. One of them was an undergraduate. He had been brought to Ebiyemiju's place after he stripped off his clothes during an examination. He then ran out of the examination hall and it took a large posse of brave men to track him down after he went to ground in the surrounding bushes. They dragged him to the Health Centre where he was heavily sedated. His people brought him posthaste to Ebiyemiju, but rumours had it that his father had calmly left instructions that his son be put down should his condition turn out to be serious. It may be coincidental that the fellow died within a week of his being admitted, but it looked suspiciously like an execution to me.

'You may wonder about the conversations, which I used to have with my brother and which led to my being incarcerated in that awful place. It is ironic that they stopped within a couple of days of my being placed in Ebiyemiju's care. All my mental powers at the time were concentrated on my own survival and I had none to spare for any extra-terrestrial conversations. I was not even aware for a long time that my brother was no longer getting through to me. By then, I could not be bothered about anything except getting out of that hole. Not long after this, I informed Ebiyemiju about my inability to hear my brother any more thinking that it would lead to my discharge. Ebiyemiju's response was a hearty laughter.

' "You think I was born yesterday?" was his scornful retort. "I have been treating madmen before you were even thought of and by now, I know all their tricks. Don't try to be smart with me, or you will live to regret it", he concluded sternly. And that was that.

'What more could I do? I was well and truly stumped, left high and dry, without any hope of an early release, or indeed, any release at all.'

Throughout this recital, Ade kept his eyes resolutely fixed on a point slightly to the left of my right eye so that there was little eye contact between us. At the beginning, I was a little disconcerted by this and wondered why he adopted this style. Then it dawned on me that he simply wanted to pour out his woes into an ear, any ear at all and since mine was within reach, it would do. As far as he was concerned, he was speaking into a microphone so to say. I fell in with his unexpressed wishes by paying close attention to what he was saying without interrupting his torrent of words by asking questions. Fortunately, I did not even need to probe with questions as Ade himself anticipated any questions and was usually able to manage to sort out my unspoken queries. At this point in the story, I began to wonder if he was just abandoned by his people and would have put the question to him. I had hardly formed the question in my mind when Ade's eyes shifted their focus from whatever was holding their attention and established eye contact. I was startled when his next words were an answer to this question.

'You may be wondering about what my people were doing about me all throughout this dark period. You can imagine that in the early period of my incarceration that I could not think of my father and grandmother without boiling with fierce anger. Then, when my anger faded as it was bound to do, I began to worry about them. After all they were my only hope of getting out of that place alive. My father came to see me on a couple of occasions bringing me news of home. On each occasion, Ebiyemiju told him that although I was improving, I was still a long way from being cured. Besides, there were other considerations.

' "You have to be patient," he counselled my worried father. "It is true that we are making progress with your son, but we must not rush anything. The forces we are battling with now realise that they have met their match. However, they are not going to give up easily and I don't blame them because your son is a good habitat for them."

' "Can you tell me how longer my son will be here?" my father asked, almost in a whisper, as he ran his eyes over my emaciated body.

' "That I cannot say precisely. You should be happy that he is getting better. Let us leave it at that for now."

"I know that you are doing your best, but as his father, I am very worried. Already he has lost a lot of time from his studies and..."

' "And what?" interrupted Ebiyemiju. "I have told you, and will tell you again and again, that you have to be patient. Many people have taken their wards away from here before I thought that they could do so safely. Go to Ibadan or Lagos and you will find most of them wandering the streets, their bottom exposed to the world. Madness is a delicate condition to manage and if you don't want your son to head for the streets, you are advised to do exactly what I tell you. No more, no less."

'He could see that my father was not entirely convinced that he was doing the right thing by leaving me under his care, so he went on.

' "You will have cause to be grateful to me later, I can assure you. It is not easy for anyone in your shoes to appreciate that point, but you will."

' "I hope so", said my father, giving up, as I knew he would.

' "There is one other thing", said Ebiyemiju.

' "What is that?" my father asked in considerable alarm, as if anything coming from Ebiyemiju had to be at least unpleasant, if not actually disturbing.

' "Have you thought about whom could be responsible for your son's condition? Don't tell me that you don't suspect that the world has a hand in this business. No, there is no doubt in my mind that somebody is behind your son's condition. You or the boy himself must have offended some powerful individual and unless such a person is identified, we are wasting our time and energy over this case."

' "I cannot think of any such person" was my father's thoughtful response. But Ebiyemiju was not going to be deflected from his line of thinking.

' "Aha, you may not be able to think of anyone now, but take it from me, we will not be completely safe until we know who controls the spirits now tormenting your son. We may even be able to turn them around so that they will not be homeless after they may have been ejected from their present quarters. Take it from me, those evil messengers must have to be sent back to whoever sent them to your son in the first place."

'My father's response was characteristically non-committal.

' "I will think about it", were his last words on the subject.

'Every job if you look hard enough has some hazard attached to it even though some are more obviously hazardous than others. As you can guess, looking after lunatics is not one of the jobs that you can feel safe in doing. Some of the patients in Ebiyemiju's care were so violent that they had to be heavily sedated and manacled before they could be approached with any degree of safety. Some others were full of diabolical cunning and had to be closely watched. They were probably more dangerous than those who were frankly violent. One minute, they are holding an intelligent conversation with you and the next, they have a heavy club in their hand and trying their best to beat out your brains. To keep that one safe step ahead of their charges, asylum attendants have to be constantly vigilant, and even then, they must have it at the back of their mind that it is simply impossible to be too careful.

'Jolly was perhaps the most dangerous person in that nest of dangerous lunatics. He was not only cunning, he was capable of generating an astonishing level of sudden, unprovoked and devastating violence. Little men, sane or insane, are quite capable of being violent, but it is a big man on the rampage who can strike real terror into all those within his reach. And Jolly was a big man, tall, broad and impressively muscled. His beady eyes, nearer the colour of blazing embers than a ripe palm-fruit, peeped on the world through a thick mat of hair which reached beyond his broad shoulders. Most times, he was as docile as a lamb, but as soon as the spirit moved him, he had to be heavily drugged and chained hand and foot to minimise damage.

'As far as Ebiyemiju was concerned, Jolly was a challenge to his skills as a healer. If he could make Jolly fit for society again, then he could lay claims to being the leading authority in the management of insanity. He wanted this primacy acknowledged and looked up to Jolly to secure it for him. He was therefore personally responsible for his star patient. Ebiyemiju himself administered all potions necessary to the patient and he only allowed his assistants to be mere lookers-on whenever he was busy with Jolly. Unfortunately, Ebiyemiju's preferred method for the management of all conditions was extremely brutal, flogging being the most prominent feature of treatment. He beat us with canes soaked in medicinal concoctions, which to my mind, only made them supple and improved their capacity to inflict pain, stinging pain, which brought hot tears to the eyes of the strongest men.

'Jolly was flogged severely and often. He was made to swallow large quantities of vile concoctions and from time to time put on starvation rations. All to no avail. He remained resolutely mad. On the other hand, Ebiyemiju was no less resolute in his determination to win lasting fame (and fortune) by caging and indeed, taming a raging tiger. Thus, their relationship was determined by a titanic battle of wills and marked by a macabre fascination one for the other. They each seemed to sparkle in each other's company since they were both aware of the danger, which one represented to the other. Theirs was a love-hate relationship. They watched each other like the proverbial hawk, trying to find the fatal chink in each other's armour through which to strike a decisive blow. The movements in this dance of death were never pretty, but were compelling in their fascination.

'The period just before sunset found most of us in Ebiyemiju's large courtyard. This was the most peaceful part of the day and each of us in his own way, enjoyed this period during which we sat in contemplation or conversed with our friends as best as we could. Ebiyemiju usually sat in one corner of the courtyard, smoking his pipe, receiving reports from his aides, holding consultations with other healers who had come to study his brutal methods, or preparing plant and animal potions.

'In the days leading to their last fateful encounter, Jolly had been on his best behaviour. He was the model of soberness, performing tasks allotted to him, swallowing all the noxious potions prescribed for him without a murmur and holding intelligible conversations with everybody including Ebiyemiju. Such behaviour could not pass unnoticed and Ebiyemiju could not help thinking that maybe, he was on the verge of a great victory. Indeed, the egotist in him must have thought that his greatest triumph was at hand. He was at this time, more relaxed and expansive than I had ever seen him to be.

'This day, Ebiyemiju was in his usual place cutting up some knotty roots into small pieces with a thick machete of extraordinary sharpness when Jolly, for once without his manacles, shuffled up to him, dragging the statutory log of wood in his wake. I was too far away to hear their conversation but from where I sat, I could see that they were having a conversation. There was nothing strange about that and I was getting up to talk to someone on the other side of the courtyard, when, out of the corner of my eye I saw Jolly suddenly stoop and give Ebiyemiju a tremendous blow, right on the solar plexus. The wind was audibly forced out of his gaping mouth and the machete flew out of his hand. Jolly's hand was on the lethal weapon in a flash and as he straightened out of his stoop, he flicked the machete sideways and decapitated his tormentor with that single blow. We were all stunned by the suddenness of this mad act and watched in horror as Ebiyemiju's head rolled away from his trunk, from which a powerful crimson jet shot out as if fired from a cannon. A pin would have been heard to fall in the eerie silence, which replaced the horrible gurgling sound, which filled the courtyard immediately after Ebiyemiju's head was parted from his body.

'We all hated Ebiyemiju, but the emotion, which attached itself to each one of us, was fear, naked and terrible fear. Jolly was bathed in bright arterial blood and he was doing a curious dance on the puddle of blood at his feet, waving his machete in the air, rather like a victorious boxer dancing a jig round the ring, his bloody gloves held aloft. The situation was horrifying. There we were, scores of people, who could not walk fast, let alone run, at the mercy of a raving lunatic in possession of the sharpest machete you ever saw, a lunatic who had just cut off one head and was bathing in fresh, warm blood. As things turned out, we did not have anything to fear. Jolly was interested in only one person. True, he danced in his victim's blood. True, he exulted in his gory victory, but he wanted only one head and no other. The euphoria of victory lasted only a short while and to the amazement of everyone, Jolly put aside his weapon and stretching his massive frame next to Ebiyemiju's lifeless body, he fell fast asleep.'

The silence after this narrative was the deepest that I had ever experienced. I could not take my eyes from Ade's face, which for the first time that night appeared to be in a state of calmness. After all that, there was really nothing more to be said. We both got up and walked out of the bar, which at that time of the night was now quite empty.

Reluctant Farmer

I carry a heavy burden of guilt with me even though I am not really sure that I committed any crime, any major crime that is. There is nobody outside the pages of a book that has not committed one minor crime or the other and I cannot even think that life is possible without the encouragement which less than serious crimes provide to the will to stay alive. So, I don't mean crime in the sense of telling the odd little lie every now and then. Or stealing a few odds and ends from people who can very well afford to live and live very comfortably in spite of the loss, which my minor larceny has inflicted on them. No, when I talk about a crime, or in this case, the crime, I mean a serious crime, one that is well worth staying awake at night to ponder over. I mean murder!

Yes, I mean murder, even though it was a murder for which an offensive weapon will never be implicated, for the simple reason that one does not exist. Sherlock Holmes may, given all the facts of the case, with more than a little dose of luck, come to the conclusion that murder had been committed. I doubt that any other detective, fictional or not, would have been able to give serious consideration to the possibility of foul play. I can indeed go further to challenge any pathologist to prove beyond reasonable doubt that my uncle was murdered. To all intents and purposes, the man died of natural causes. A prominent pathologist subjected his body to detailed post-mortem examination and no mysterious puncture marks were found on his plump body. No known poison was found in any part of his body and of course no rude lesions were present. Instead, the old fellow died with a beatific smile on his face and departed apparently without malice towards anybody, man, woman or child. But, all these are no consolation to me. You see, I think I killed him. I come from a village in the very heart of Nigeria. I will not say more than that for fear that somebody who knows me would put two and two together and come up with the right answer. Not that I really mind being fingered, but not in this way. The point is that I want to tell a story and the earlier I started the better.

In a part of the world where the only respectable occupation was farming, my uncle was a civil servant. He did not pretend to be involved in the taking of vital government decisions, but there was no doubt that he enjoyed being close, at least physically to the seat of so much power. He had not bothered to fill his head with more than a smattering of knowledge but he could, given time write a few sentences in a fair hand and read the obituaries in the newspapers, especially when they were adorned with large photographs. Nevertheless, he knew enough to land a job with the government and keep it over a very long period of time during which he knew the bosses he enjoyed talking to us about several, no, many times. It seemed to me at least, that the only permanent feature in the civil service was my unassuming uncle.

When my uncle joined the civil service some forty years before the start (the proper start, that is) of this story, he was blazing a trail, a narrow one it must be said, but a trail all the same for the people of our village. The trail was narrow out of necessity because it was several years after he took the plunge that anyone else did the same. Now however, with a significant number of people from our village in paid employment, my uncle is a celebrity, his modest exploits now part of the clan's legends.

As with all legends, the beginning was rough, very rough indeed. To start with, the poor man did not have his father's blessing and although this may not be of importance to people in other places, in our village, it was a tragedy to be scrupulously avoided. Parents were venerated in our neck of the woods and for the first male child to leave home without the consent of his father was tantamount to a renunciation of all his rights within the family. In leaving home therefore, my uncle was leaving something precious behind. Many years later, my uncle confessed that he was very nearly dissuaded from leaving home at the time by his father's opposition, but he went on all the same to escape from the life of a farmer which he described as brutal and grossly underprivileged.

'I hated farming with a passion almost as soon as I was introduced to it as a boy' he told me one day as we sat drinking palm-wine under the shade of a huge mango tree in front of his house in the village. In those days, my uncle's habits were governed by moderation and it must not be thought that it was the wine that was bubbling to the surface as speech. He was stone sober and talked to me only because he wanted to keep a conversation going between us. Wine goes down better when there are words for company.

'Yes' he said, and repeated for emphasis, 'I hated farming right from the start. Look at this village. The place is full of farmers, their overworked wives and numerous children, all of them battling with mind-bending poverty. True they get to eat what in town will be described as prodigious meals, most of the people here look pitifully undernourished.

'They eat the same unappetising mess each day and then work, or rather, slave all day on the farm from the crack of dawn. At the end of the planting season, they get little more than what they put into the ground at the beginning. For one thing, there is always one thing or the other wrong with the weather. The rains either come early, or too late, and sometimes, not at all. There should not be rain during the harvest, but you can be sure that as soon as it is time to fetch in the crops, it would start to pour for days on end and the harvest spoilt. Even when the harvest is good, they are still in trouble with pests, sharp businessmen who cheat them at every turn and numerous creditors snapping around their ankles and every now and then, administering a painful nip, just to keep them in line.'

'Come, come uncle', I interjected, 'it can't be as bad as that. Surely, there must be something to be said for farming or else our people would not have been devoted to it for so many generations.'

'Devoted or not, my picture is as accurate as any picture can be. Our people have remained farmers only because they cannot summon up the mental energy to do something more profitable. Nobody should be devoted to such a thankless exercise as farming. Even for our people, farmers as they are, it is still something to be endured.'

'Surely, something that is endured throughout life by one generation after another has become part of culture and tradition.'

'And who says that culture is not just something to be endured? There are so many aspects of our culture that are either pointless or downright unpalatable that were they not to be artfully imposed, much of what we call our culture would have long been thrown overboard.'

'Now uncle,' I pleaded, 'don't let us take a detour through the wilderness of culture.'

'But you started it' my uncle retorted. 'I was content to talk about farming which I insist is a form of torture.'

'A form of torture, which gives us food' I reminded him.

'Food, yes. I have no difficulty with that. What I insist upon is that someone other than me should do the farming. All other members of my age-group society are farmers and believe me, I don't like them any less for it.'

As if on cue, three members of his age-group society made a noisy entrance at this point and I had to leave them to their own devices.

Uncle knew from the start that his escape route from the farm was the classroom. He was about eleven years old when some enterprising missionaries in the next village some five kilometres away, opened a school of sorts. Attending the school therefore meant a ten-kilometre trek every school day.

'The distance was no problem' insisted Uncle. 'In those days, we went everywhere on foot and saw a motorised vehicle in our neck of the woods two or three times a year. Five kilometres was a warming-up distance for people who regularly travelled the forty-five kilometres between here and the nearest railway station with bags of groundnuts on their heads.'

Most of the pupils in the school were the children of people from other parts of the country. They had been part of work-gangs, which had laid the railway track all the way up from the coast. Some of them had felt that our area was a good place to settle down in and had gone back home to bring wives by whom they had children who needed to go to school. Although there had been some mixing over the years, the two groups, that is, the indigenes and the migrants are still quite distinct. Many of those who had been in school with my uncle had found the village too cramped and had either gone to the town like my uncle, or back to the places from where their parents had migrated. Those of them who stayed on in the village were mainly traders and artisans, selling everything from needles to motorcycles and keeping all items of machinery in the village, adequately maintained. I knew for a fact that, but for these people, the grains produced by the villagers would have remained unground since they operated all the mills with which the grains were reduced to powder.

Unfortunately, Uncle did not find learning very easy. By his own ready admission, virtually everything connected with books and learning was painfully strange to him. All he had going for him was a dogged determination not to become a farmer. As soon as he passed his first school-leaving certificate (on the second attempt) he shook the dust of school from his feet and headed for the wide open spaces of the nearest town which fortunately, was a provincial capital with jobs on offer for the likes of him.

Going off to town was however, a difficult proposition. It was unheard of for a young, able-bodied and apparently full-blooded male of his generation to turn his back on a farming career for what was disdainfully dismissed as a life of riot and debauchery in town. It was fortunate that he was not female, as everyone would have concluded that a life of prostitution was the attraction. On second thoughts, it may have made matters simpler if he was female because some people were wondering if he did not need careful watching since the only occupation open to young men in towns, at least in their dim imagination, was stealing.

My uncle did not care what anyone thought of him. He just had to get away and he did.

All the foregoing considered, it must come as something of a shock when I say that I am struggling to put down these lines in the shade of a tree on my uncle's farm. I cannot think of any greater irony than that. My uncle went away to town and by the standards of the day, he was an unqualified success. The people in our village became aware of his true potential on the day he rode into the village on a brand new bicycle, courtesy of a loan from his employers. Nobody in the village had performed such a feat before and he became an instant celebrity.

'That bicycle was easily the most profitable investment that I ever made' Uncle graciously conceded on one of my numerous visits to him.

'You see, keen as I was to get away from my father's farm and the village, in that order, I had no idea whatsoever about what living in a town was like. It did not take me long to find out. Indeed, I was up against it right from the very first day. I had no friends, relations or even acquaintances living in the town at that time, so I was completely on my own. I slept in the courtyard of some rich man for the first few days and at least that gave me some breathing space. What I had not prepared for, was the loneliness. True I was one of several dozen people taking refuge in that compound but I had never felt so lonely in all my life.

'The loneliness of a town has a cruel quality not to be matched anywhere else except in a bigger town. You see people all around you but they may just as well not be there for the attention you get from them. You can see but cannot touch or be touched and without touching the human spirit withers and dies. It becomes brittle and crumbles into the dust, never to be put together again. Being alone in a big town is rather like being thirsty on a small island with water all around you. Salt water, which you dare not put to your lips.'

'And yet you stayed on in town when the logical thing for you to do was tó go back home.'

'I had my pride to think of. I had my pride. It did not cross my mind for one idle moment to go back home. I had burnt my boats when I spurned the sound advice given to me with due solemnity by my father and uncles that I stayed at home. To run back to the village after a few days or even months would have been too humiliating and being young, I thought that I would rather die than eat humble pie. The words, "I told you so" were re-echoing in my head in those days and I knew that I could not bear to hear them uttered by my father.'

'In any case, you survived.'

'You bet I did. In the first place, I was most fortunate to get a job right away. I was employed as a messenger and general dogsbody to the District Officer, my predecessor in that post having had a fatal encounter with a viper in the course of his duties. He had died only a couple of days before I presented myself at the District Secretariat in the faint hope that I could be given a job. I was paid the princely sum of ten shillings every month.'

'Ten shillings!' I whistled in disbelief. 'That is hardly enough to buy a decent orange these days.'

'In those days, it was a fortune. It was such a large sum that it convinced me straightaway of the correctness of my decision about turning my back on farming. More than this it made me think that I could get married on it and thereby solve that nagging problem of loneliness. That is something to be said about money. As soon as you have a few pennies in your pocket, the urge to spend them, wisely or otherwise is overwhelming. As far as I was concerned, I had money to spend, or burn as the case may be and I needed a wife. Marrying costs money and the obvious thing was to part with some money and get a wife in return.'

'But did you not have to find a wife first?'

My uncle looked at me in genuine surprise, as if I had said something that could not be believed.

You know, it is really difficult for people of my generation to appreciate how much things have changed from our days until when people like you ask questions like this.'

My puzzlement deepened.

'What does my question have to do with generational changes?' I wanted to know.

'It seems that you are genuinely ignorant, so I have to educate you after all. In those days, it was not the problem of a young man to find himself a wife. That duty was left to his father. All a son had to do was tell his father whenever he was ready for the responsibility of looking after a wife. If the father was convinced that the son had demonstrated his ability to support a wife, he did his duty by the son and duly obliged him by presenting him with a suitable wife. At least as far as the first wife was concerned.'

'I see' I responded, even though I did not think that there was anything for me to see. It sounded strange to me that a man could leave the delicate process of finding a wife to another man, even if the other man was his own father. Not wanting to task my uncle's patience, I kept these thoughts to myself and allowed him to get on with his story.

'I went back to the village six months after I left to tell my father that I was ready for a wife.'

'Was he pleased that you had settled down so soon?' I asked.

'To tell the truth, I thought he would be, but I was wrong. He just laughed derisively and asked how I intended to support a wife. He wanted to know how many heaps of yams I had planted that season. He did not think that there was any man alive who would willingly sentence his daughter to a life of certain starvation by marrying her off to me and having her go off to a strange place to boot. He even went on for good measure to tell me that if I was not his son and somebody had approached him on my behalf, he would not entertain my suit for a second. You can imagine that this response brought me back to earth with an almighty bump. It made me realise that I had to show concrete evidence of my new affluence to the people in the village, or else, they would continue to think that I was lazy and good for nothing.'

'Uncle, I am puzzled about one aspect of your story' I cut in at this point.

'Only part, or all of it?'

'Only part of it' I confirmed. 'Given the awe with which white men were regarded in those days, how come your father was not impressed by your physical closeness to the DO who, as far as the people were concerned was no less than God's own representative on earth?'

'Ah, that is a good question. It is a good question, but not good enough. You see, you have assumed that my story about working for the DO was believed. Well, it was not. My father did not waste his credulity by paying any attention to what in his estimation, was a tall tale. He simply could not imagine that I was privileged to stand in the presence of one so exalted as the DO. I am afraid, my father was ashamed of a son who not only ran away from doing a real man's job but, was telling the most awful lies to cover up. I knew that there was no way I could persuade him to give me a chance, so I changed the subject and tried not to show that I was hurt.'

The solution to this problem was to buy a bicycle, but it did not come immediately to my uncle. It would perhaps not have come at all had he not discussed his plight with his colleagues. To his surprise, he found that a couple of them, one of whom came from a village on the other side of town from ours had had to grapple with the same problem of credibility. It was he who advised my uncle to buy a bicycle.

'Even if you build a house in town, nobody will believe you, should you go back home to tell them about it' he was told.

'You have to show them something valuable, something, which will give loud testimony to your ability to acquire property and, nothing speaks louder in your favour than property. Take a bicycle home during the Christmas holidays and you are made for life.'

'But', protested my uncle, 'won't they think that I borrowed the bicycle, just to give them the impression that I had property, as you put it?'

'Use your head, my friend!' he was advised. 'How many people are in a position to borrow a bicycle to be taken the distance to your wretched little village and at Christmas too? A man who can borrow a bicycle under those circumstances must be a man of considerable worth.'

My uncle thanked his colleagues for their help and thereafter, took the decision to buy a bicycle.

Taking the decision to buy a bicycle and actually taking possession of a brand-new Raleigh, complete with a dynamo which hummed as the bicycle was pedalled along, were events which were separated by several frustrating months. The main obstacle to the achievement of the desired objective was that ancient enemy of man, time. It is either too slow or too fast and it is something that cannot be captured and put in a bag. Unless you are a usurer, you cannot get time to work for you. When you are separated by time from something desirable, it has the maddening property of slowing down to a crawl and then speeding up like a horse under the lash as soon as you settle down to enjoy the fruits of your desire. My uncle was told upon enquiries that his appointment had to be confirmed before his application for a bicycle loan could be considered and confirmation could not be effected until he had put in a year's service. Confirmation was however not automatic at the end of this period as people had been known to wait for nearly three years before their appointment was reluctantly confirmed.

There and then, my uncle decided to perform his duties so diligently that the desired confirmation of appointment would be achieved in the shortest possible time. Exactly twelve months and three weeks after he was first employed, he came to work and found a very official letter waiting for him. His heart pounding with excitement, he tore open the buff envelope and there it was, the long awaited confirmation of his humble appointment. He did not waste a minute after that but rushed off to collect the relevant forms, which, with the help of one of his better read colleagues, he filled as accurately as he could. The forms were submitted through the Chief Clerk, whose interest in the application was stimulated by the five-shilling note, which was pinned to it. The application was sent up through the bureaucratic staircase but, the five-shilling note was smartly detached and no less smartly transferred into the Chief Clerk's pocket. Thereafter, the application became his responsibility and he kept his eyes on it as it made its rounds of the various tables on which it landed in the following two weeks culminating in its final approval three weeks later. My uncle was on his way towards the big time.

'You will not believe the excitement, which was generated by my gentle and tired descent on the village on that occasion when I went home on my bicycle for the very first time.'

'Do you mean that you rode all the twenty-five kilometers to the village?'
I asked in genuine surprise.
My uncle smiled grimly.
'Going home on my bicycle was an improvement on the former mode which was on foot.'

After that triumphant entry, my uncle was the toast of the village and everyone wanted to bask in the warmth of his triumph by associating with him. Not even the girls were left out of the general adulation. Even if they could not be as effervescent as the other villagers, their flashing eyes spoke up for their approval of this young man who not only had the courage to turn his back on their world, but was already making waves in his strange new world. A wife was duly arranged for the conquering hero who promptly took her off to town, which more than ever, was now home to him.

My uncle had become a celebrity and his house gradually became the outpost of the village, the point of attraction for all those who were coming to town, some of them coming to seek their fortune in the same way as my uncle. Unfortunately, the old man did not climb the bureaucratic ladder as quickly as his exalted starting position portended. But, this did not seem to bother him as he did no more than what was expected of him. Some of his more ambitious and aggressive contemporaries took advantage of the opportunities, which were opened up by independence to occupy some pretty important positions. Not so, my uncle. His career drifted along unspectacularly but I suspect, very much to his satisfaction.

My uncle's career was a gentle drift and it mirrored his life faithfully. He did everything without fuss and it was becoming clear that he had begun to look forward to a quiet retirement, long before he was obliged to retire. Many of my uncle's contemporaries superintended a harem in their government-provided quarters. In one interesting case, four wives had to share their husband and three rooms between them, not to talk of a horde of children trying manfully to grow towards adulthood and flight from the overcrowded coop. Not so my uncle. He was apparently, happily married to Auntie Amina, a taciturn but warm lady who seemed to have less and less to say about anything as time went by and age, which gave her movements an action replay quality. The couple had three children and their house was consequently regarded as a palace, all that space for such a small family. The people from the village must have been happy about this state of affairs because it meant that they had a place to stay whenever they came to town.

About ten years to my uncle's mandatory retirement, I butted into his life. I am Auntie Amina's nephew and therefore only related to my uncle by marriage, but for all that, we were kindred spirits and spent many happy hours together chewing the fat as it were, in a way that was rather strange given the disparity in our ages.

Like my uncle I got away from the village as soon as I could. Much to my surprise, I passed the entrance examination to the Government College in town and I came up from the village. I was thirteen at the time and it was to my uncle's house that I came whenever we were given a day off from the boarding house. I looked forward very much to those outings not only because of my auntie's delicious cooking but the opportunity of conversation with my uncle. Unlike other adults in my world, he was always genuinely interested in what I thought about a wide variety of subjects and I had no doubt that he took my observations seriously. To tell the truth, I did not think of him as my uncle. He was my friend.

Like my uncle, I joined the Civil Service as soon as I could, but unlike him, I came to the Service armed with a Bachelor's degree in History and therefore started as a senior civil servant with a host of privileges. It was in the course of my duties that I became acquainted with a government scheme to give loans for agricultural projects to people who could be trusted to do something tangible for agricultural production. My department was in charge of administering the loans and the first candidate that came to my mind was my uncle. I thought that it would be a good idea for the old fellow to retire early to a farm and make some money to sweeten his later years, which God willing should be many. But, I knew that it was unlikely that my uncle was going to share my enthusiasm for this scheme especially because of his antagonism to the farming process.

I went to see my uncle as soon as it was decided to prosecute the Agricultural Loan Scheme in the same house that I used to come as a student all those years ago.

'What are your plans for retirement?' I asked my uncle as soon as we sat down in our respective favourite chairs.

'Retirement? Why should I start thinking of retirement, which is still some ten years away? There is plenty of time before then and in any case, why should I do more than retire to my house in the village and take things easy when I eventually retire. I should not need a lot of money to satisfy my modest needs.'

'Do you really think that you will be satisfied with doing nothing day after day? You will soon be bored to tears by the slow pace of life in the village.'

'That is what you think' replied my uncle. 'There are a million and one things to keep me occupied.'

'A million and one things in that place! You must be joking. Three months in the village and you will be back here like a shot.'

'We may sit here debating that point until the cows come home and not get anywhere at all. What I want to know is what you are doing to ensure that the road through our village is tarred before the next rainy season. Right now, transport operators route their vehicles away from our village and the few rickety buses that risk their nuts and bolts on our road, charge their unfortunate passengers the earth for the privilege of shaking their bones to pieces.'

'No uncle' I replied very firmly. 'I have come to see you about your retirement because the government is putting a scheme together and it is people like you who should reap the benefits which are such a prominent part of the programme.'

'Government schemes!' said my uncle, his voice dripping with acid scorn. 'Don't talk to me about government schemes. They all fail and certainly I have no intention to being part of a failure.'

'That is not fair' I cried with considerable passion. 'You have jumped to a conclusion without even bothering to hear what the scheme is all about.'

'I don't need to know a thing about this precious scheme of yours.' retorted my uncle. 'All I know is that no scheme proposed by the so-called government of this country has ever worked. Not since we became independent, that is.'

'Oh no Uncle, here you go again on your hobbyhorse, riding down all signs of reason in your way. When are you going to stop missing your departed colonial masters?'

'As long as their successors continue to make a mess of everything' replied my unrepentant uncle.

It was against this stormy background that I told my uncle about the proposed Agricultural Loan Scheme. It was designed to boost agricultural production and at the same time create a rural elite which was to bring much needed development to the countryside. In doing so, it was to slow down the rate of population drift into the towns, which were slowly filling up with all kinds of undesirable migrants. Under the scheme, loans were to be given to carefully selected individuals to set up model tree farms. A technical group had established the suitability of our area for the cultivation of citrus and mango trees. To take advantage of this, the government wanted people to plant these trees on a commercial scale. They were to supply the raw materials for a giant fruit-canning factory, which was to be built with a hefty loan from a consortium of European banks. I explained to my uncle that if he took early retirement, I was going to make sure that he got a loan to develop a hundred acres of land.

The response to my proposal was an uncharacteristic silence from my uncle.

'Well?' I asked rather tentatively. 'What do you think of it?'

'Hmm' replied my uncle. 'Fine, very fine indeed.'

'That is what I think of the scheme too, but to be honest, your endorsement of it is very far from being enthusiastic and that worries me.'

'Why should it worry you?' queried my uncle. 'All government schemes are fine, at least on paper. The trouble starts when the plan leaves the drawing board and is taken into the fields. Then, everything, which can go wrong, duly does so and before you know it, the whole thing is in tatters and the air is thick with recriminations, broken promises and painful regrets. No my boy, count me out of any government scheme. I know too much about the government to put any trust in anything concocted by government officials. Take my word for it, as long as you bright young men are running the show, nobody should invest any trust in any government scheme.'

To say that I was shocked by this brutal assessment from a veteran of the Civil Service would be a gross understatement of my feelings.

'How can you say these things for goodness sake!' I exploded. 'You know just how hard we work and...'

'I know how hard you bosses work alright' my uncle interrupted forcefully. 'There is no denying that you all work very hard. It is just that all you do is use government apparatus to achieve your own private ends. The scheme will work for as long as you are making huge profits for yourselves and since most of you are not content with just the golden eggs, you will not rest until the wretched goose is butchered and that is it. Finished!'

I was stumped. Could this be my uncle? Could this be the unflappable civil servant who throughout his working life had been carrying out government orders to the best of his ability? I mean, the fellow could be nothing but a rabid revolutionary. At least that is what flashed through my mind as I gazed in wonder at my uncle who repaid me gaze for gaze, apparently without any misgivings. I sank back in my chair the better to absorb the shock. But it was no use. I was shaken to the very depths of my soul.

'How can you continue to do your work with equanimity given the feelings which you have about the people who run the service?'

My uncle let off a harsh laugh.

'One thing which working in the Civil Service has taught me is that I should not allow my personal feelings to interfere with my official duties. I know that the Civil Service is full of scoundrels, but what can I do about it? I carry on with my humble duties and leave the worrying to the eggheads.'

Conversation would have been difficult after this but for the fact that Auntie Amina called out that supper was served. I was very pleased about this, not just because it saved me from considerable embarrassment but because we were invited to do justice to a steaming bowl of *amala*, my favourite food. *Amala* is a Yoruba invention and I had acquired the taste for it when I was an undergraduate at Ibadan and was delighted to find that my auntie had learnt how to make *amala* from some of her Yoruba friends right there in our village. Unfortunately, my wife had never learnt what it took to make a great dish of *amala* and my auntie always gave me a treat in the shape of *amala* as often as she could.

Auntie's *amala* was even better than usual that day and I enjoyed it immensely even as I pondered my uncle's words in my mind. I decided that there was no trying to get him to look at things from my own point of view, at least not then. I thought that I should beat a strategic retreat in order to be able to resume the fight at some other time. I was determined to win the war however because I believed sincerely that the Agricultural Loan Scheme was an important component of development as I saw it and the people who could make the scheme work were those like my uncle who were both hardworking and reliable. Indeed without people like him, the scheme was bound to fail and fail dismally. We just had to make the scheme work if we were not to build a culture of failure.

For the next couple of months, I wore down my uncle's resistance to the Loan Scheme with the persistence of water eroding hard rock. I pointed out all the advantages of the scheme and freely invented others, which of course, existed only in my fertile imagination. When in the end I was able to convince my uncle of the soundness of the scheme, I found that a great deal of his resistance to the scheme was the need to retire from the service. He had become as comfortable with the routines of his job that leaving it for something, which he was not completely convinced of its merits, filled him with dread. He simply did not have the nerve to cut himself off from his surrogate mother, the mighty Civil Service. He needed the security which the service represented in the same way as a baby needed its mother's milk.

Had I not been able to persuade my uncle to participate in the Agricultural Loan Scheme, I would not have been able to tell this story. The long and short of the matter of it all is that my uncle finally succumbed to my pressures and agreed to take the loan and early retirement.

This particular loan was processed even faster than the famous bicycle loan that made it possible for my uncle to acquire a wife.

Unknown to my uncle, I had identified a piece of land for his farm, long before he agreed to participate in the scheme which is another reason why I was determined to get him to say yes. The site, which I chose after very careful deliberation, was nearly 25 kilometres from our village, a distance, which could be covered easily especially since part of the loan was for the purchase of a small but sturdy van. I had taken great care to secure a place, which I was sure my uncle was going to find irresistible. I was very pleased therefore when the old fellow fell in love with the place as soon as he saw it. By that time, the site had been cleared and made ready to receive the thousands of mango seedlings, which were soon to be planted on it.

When I took my uncle to see the site for the first time, the wily old fox tried to be casual about the whole thing, but it was clear that he was in the grip of some excitement. In the end his enthusiasm got the better of him.

'This is a grand place for a tree farm' he burst out at last. It was clear that his aversion for farming was still with him. He made the comment that had his father had the opportunity of planting thousands of mango trees on such a site as he was presented with, he probably would not have run away from home and farm as he did all those many years ago. 'This is a grand place for a tree farm and one should be able to reap bountiful harvests from it' he reiterated, on completion of his tour of inspection.

'That is the idea Uncle, that is the idea. This area has been found by the experts to be perfect for the cultivation of citrus and mango trees. We want as many people as possible to take advantage of this gift of nature. It is all right to plant yams and millet here but, to make real money, we have to plant fruit trees. Our people may not appreciate the value of fruits because we are surrounded by all sorts of fruit trees, which are apparently growing wild. But there are other places where fruits are almost priceless and we can take advantage of the high prices in those places by sending the fruits harvested on farms like this over there and of course to the fruit-canning factory which the government is now building very near here.'

My uncle was pleased to see his farm site but he was overjoyed to receive the money to set things rolling. And when he took possession of his van, he was clearly over the moon. It seemed that everything had come good for my uncle because the cheque for his gratuity payment came right on the heels of his van and suddenly, the old man had more money in his hot little hands than he had ever had to hope for. Now all he had to do was spend it. And how he spent it!

I had thought that my uncle would live in his old house in the village and commute to the farm as often as he needed to. He had other ideas. As soon as the money hit his pocket, he decided that he needed a house right there on the farm and straightaway, made plans to have one built. It was a modest house but with all the modern conveniences without which my uncle regarded his life as empty. The house took a hefty bite out of his gratuity, but it was well worth it if only because of the joy, which the old fellow took in his little house.

The first sign of trouble was that when the house was ready, my uncle moved into it by himself leaving Auntie Amina behind in the village. The ostensible reason for this was that it would not be fair to Auntie if she was taken away from the village so soon after her return from the town. To tell the truth, Auntie Amina was quite pleased with this arrangement. Her children had left home and she had a lot of time on her hands, time which she could spend enjoyably with her friends and relatives in the village. All through her stay in town, she regarded her absence from home as an extended sabbatical and she was most anxious to get back to the life she knew in those far-off premarital days.

Uncle's house on the farm was in the beginning, a bachelor pad. Its choice location and Uncle's ready hospitality soon made the place a cynosure. It seemed at least to me, that the place was always crowded out with all manner of people, sitting in the shade of a large neem tree in front of the house with the inevitable gourd of fresh palm-wine in the middle.

'This is th' fe' my uncle told me over and over again, his shiny face beaming like a powerful beacon. 'I don't know how I survived in the closeness of town for such a long time. Just look at this view. Enchanting, don't you think?'

On one of my visits I noticed that my host was in a rather pensive mood. It looked like he was only present before me in the flesh, his mind having wandered way over the horizon.

'What is on your mind?' I was forced to ask at last.

'Well', began Uncle rather tentatively and then stopped

'Well, what?' I wanted to know.

'I am thinking of a rather delicate matte and I am not sure whether I should seek your opinion or not.'

'You know you can count on me to help you in any situation, Uncle, at least as long as I am in a position to be helpful.'

My uncle gave me a level look as if sizing me up, weighing my capacity for executing the job in hand.

'You know my friend Abdu' he said at last.

I nodded assent.

'He came here with a curious proposition this morning and I am still trying to work out an appropriate answer.'

'What kind of proposition is that?'

'Let me tell you what happened' suggested my uncle.

I sat back to listen.

'Abdu came here this morning bright and early. He was on his way to the farm and so he did not have all the time in the world. He had barely sat down when he asked for your auntie. I found that very strange because he knew very well that your auntie stays in the village. With a little thought however I decided that it was a tricky question and waited patiently for him to come to the point he set out to make all along. He then told me that at my age, I needed a wife who would be at my beck and call and the sooner I acquired one, the better. "What about my wife, Amina?" I asked him.

' "Call Amina, a wife!" he replied hooting with laughter. "Don't make me laugh", he went on even though he had barely recovered from a paroxysm of laughter. "Her primary responsibility is now to her children and I can assure you that she has little or no time for you. The point is, as things stand now, you are an embarrassment to me and I intend to send one of my daughters to you before the end of the week. Get ready for the wedding."

'He actually told me about preparing for a wedding over his shoulder because he was already on his way out of the house as he put forward his proposition...'

'You can't be serious' I said as I tried to suppress the snort of laughter that was threatening to tear me apart. In the end, I gave in to it and laughed loud and long.

'What is so funny?' my uncle asked.

'You becoming a groom now is certainly very funny' I replied. 'And if you marry a young woman, we can expect a baby or two very soon.'

My uncle gave me a withering look.

'I thought you of all people will have the sense to see the serious side of this issue. What do I want with a young wife at this time?'

'You must look at this situation from a positive side', I advised. 'A young wife will keep you very much interested in life. She will give you that spark, which will make you get up and go. Frankly, I think that the suggestion is very sound and I must say, I am firmly in support of it.'

Abdu was not a man to take no for an answer or allow the grass to grow under his feet and the proposed wedding was speedily contracted and consummated. True to my prediction, a baby duly arrived within the year.

In the meantime, Uncle's farm was taking shape. More than 90% of the seedlings that had been planted had taken root and begun to put up impressive foliage. Things were looking up very much indeed which is probably why yet another of his friends presented another bride to him. A man of his stature, it was reasoned, needed several wives to properly reflect his exalted status. My uncle had become noticeably uxorious since he got married to his young wife and the second one was welcomed with something close to enthusiasm.

Understandably perhaps, my uncle began to spend less time with his trees and kept to the shade as much as possible whenever he went out to inspect them. He needed a great deal of strength and stamina for conjugal activities and so, he husbanded whatever strength and stamina he had very carefully. It was however plain that the old man was indeed enjoying himself. He became noticeably more relaxed, easy going and pleasant. He was ever solicitous of his young wives and tried to make them as comfortable as they wished to be. Perhaps this is why another young lady was added to the harem. It was a lucky thing that there were no more than four rooms in uncle's house, or else, who knows, other young ladies would have been attracted to the stable.

There could be no doubt that my uncle was a happy man in those days. His wives spoilt him. He was fed like a prize animal and his every wish was attended to with dispatch. At an age when he should have been playing with his grandchildren, he was romping around with his second batch of children. And as far as my uncle was concerned, it was all due to me.

'If you had not approved of Abdu's proposition, I would not have accepted his generous offer' my uncle informed me. 'I was counting on you to show me the way through and as things stand, I should be very grateful to you.'

'Mind you' he went on, I think three wives are a bit too much to handle, but I think I am doing okay' he concluded with a smirk.

He was certainly doing okay, but not as well as he thought, because only two weeks later, he was dead. Dead of heart failure.

The story, as such stories are, was confused. He had slept in the bed of his wife number 3 (or is it 4, counting Auntie Amina) but had returned to his room sometime before dawn without disturbing his companion. He did not respond to the call for breakfast.

Uncle's farm is doing very well indeed. The canning factory is not doing so well. As my uncle predicted, it was never commissioned. Someone had made off with the money set aside for it. Still, the scheme was not the total failure that my uncle feared it would be. People came from far and near to purchase the fruits even before they were ripe for plucking and so the money came in a steady stream. With the farm doing so well, uncle's young family is being very well-looked after and I am happy about that. It is just that I often wonder if I did not have something to do with my uncle's sudden demise.

Missing Persons

There is no way of knowing that the man lying in the much rumpled hospital bed was a young man barely into his forties. A sudden and particularly virulent illness had, within three pain-filled weeks, wracked his frame, destroyed his youthfulness and precipitated an irreversible plunge into extreme old age. He lay on his bed and took long, shuddering breaths at infrequent intervals, trying to force life back into a body on the verge of surrender. His bony hands roved all over his emaciated body as if to put out the fires which were raging furiously at the very core of his being. Two electric fans on either side of the bed were working frantically to bring much needed relief, but they worked in vain as the fever consuming his flesh was so deep-seated that the breezes generated did not do more than bounce off his unresponsive skin. Not even the powerful drugs with which he was being recklessly dosed could quench the fires, which were raging through his body.

In spite of his desperate condition however, he had not yet been driven to the point of loosening his tenacious, but apparently futile hold on life. He had not yet been led to the point of no return where the desire to find relief in death becomes stronger than the will to live, even though, to remain alive was to take terrific punishment, very likely, to no purpose. Tolu was still hoping for a recovery, a miraculous recovery, but a recovery all the same. Even as the fires raged unchecked through his battered body, his determination not to go under was unquenched and as pain gripped him like a giant vice, he looked forward from time to time to a calm period of wholesomeness and banished pain.

'I am too young to die', his mind kept saying to him. 'My mother, old as she is, is still very much alive, so what business do I have with death? My father died at eighty, and one of my uncles is still alive at an age very close to ninety. No, this cannot be the end. My children need me too much for me to give up at this point in time. I simply must not let go.'

Tolu's optimism was justified, or at least not entirely misplaced as he had on two previous occasions been hauled back from the very edge of the grave. What he was refusing to acknowledge however was that his body, dangerously weak from earlier attacks was in a much weaker position from which to keep death at bay. He was still determined to keep a grip on life, no matter how tenuous it was, but what he was not aware of, was his body's desire for terminal rest. His major organs which had stood up manfully to the relentless assault of enforced malfunction were, even at that time in the middle of a grand conspiracy to engineer a shutdown of all vital processes as that was to be his very last day alive.

Tolu's wife, Moji was constantly at his bedside. The nurses on the ward had become accustomed to seeing her buxom figure seated stolidly by her husband, sponging down his burning forehead and dispensing words of encouragement. She left the ward very close to midnight every day, just before the very last bus she could take, departed from the bus-stop in front of the hospital. No matter how late she stayed however, she was back at the crack of dawn, her determination to help her husband fight death, plainly visible on her face.

Death, when it finally came for Tolu was mercifully swift. He had not had time to contemplate his own mortality when his heart failed. The heart which for a little more than forty years had, under the influence of measured electrical impulses pumped blood through his whole body, went berserk and totally out of all forms of control. The muscles of his left ventricle, which had contracted and relaxed rhythmically all his life, lost that all-important rhythm and began to writhe ineffectually like a bowl of fat worms. The same effect would have been obtained by a shot through the heart. He was dead within seconds.

Shortly afterwards, the nurse on the ward discovered, in between naps, that the patient in bed No 14 was dead. As far as she was concerned, this was something of an inconvenience since it gave her a few things to do. Things she would rather not be doing as all around her, the world lay fast asleep.

First, she had to find a doctor who was to certify that the patient was really dead and not just pretending to be so. Then, screened from her sleeping charges, she was to pack the corpse, ready for dispatch to the mortuary. She went about her tasks, not with a will, but with competence born by repetition. It was as if she was on automatic pilot so that it was after the body had been delivered to the mortuary that she allowed her mind to once again relate her activities.

'Poor woman' she sighed as her thoughts were fastened on Moji who had been left with the responsibility of bringing up four children by herself. 'Poor woman, she is really up against it. Things were difficult enough before, but now, they are going to be really rough and tough. Oh, I sincerely hope that she won't come before I go off duty because I don't think I can handle having to tell her about her loss.'

Moji came in bright and early as usual, but that day, an experienced nurse was waiting for her.

'Good-morning. Mrs. Ojo' the nurse called out as soon as Moji's frame darkened the entrance to the ward.

'Good-morning, ma' responded Moji as she curtsied in deference to the nurse's age and position.

'How are the children?'

'They are fine, ma, we thank God.'

'Good, very good' beamed the nurse and then went on, 'I am afraid you can't see your husband this morning. He has been taken to the laboratory for some tests, which will take all morning.

'What kind of tests are those?' Moji asked in sudden alarm. 'I was not told about them yesterday.'

'Nobody knew that the tests would be done this morning because Dr Akande, the Consultant conducting the tests decided at the last minute to do them and since his unit is very busy the doctors looking after your husband decided that the opportunity should not be missed. Don't worry. By the time you come back this afternoon, you will be able to see your husband and the doctors will be in a better position to give him proper treatment. Go home and come back later this afternoon.'

Moji's initial reaction was to reject this piece of advice, but it sounded too much like an order from a person with authority for it not to be given serious consideration and so on second thoughts, she decided to go back home, to await the coming of the afternoon. Then, she could return to resume her vigil by her husband's bed.

Moji went back home, her mind in a whirl. She hoped that the new tests would make it possible for the doctors to do something for her husband. When she stepped into the house however, she knew instinctively that she had become a widow. Crammed into their tiny sitting room were her in-laws and parish priest, all of them very grim and deathly quiet.

'Oh, my God!' she shouted as the priest moved towards her. 'It is all over for me. Oh God, what am I to do? Tell me. Tell me that my husband is not dead' she pleaded. 'He can't be dead' she screamed as she looked from one face to the other, trying to find a denial in at least one of them. What she saw in each one was a confirmation of her worst fears as tears began to course down every cheek within her range of vision. Any lingering doubt was removed when the priest, taking her in his arms informed her as gently as he could that the Lord had indeed taken her husband onto himself.

'He has gone to be with his maker and although we are weeping today, we should indeed be joyful because as Christians we know that death is not the end. It is indeed the beginning. Our brother has started a new life, a life of joy in the Lord', concluded the priest in practised tones.

Moji wanted desperately to believe what the priest was saying, but in the end, she rejected the "goodness of the Lord" and asked in a loud voice why God had chosen to take her husband, leaving her children fatherless. Even in her grief, she was not deserted by her commonsense. She wanted to know from the servant of God in front of her how on earth she was going to look after the children all by herself. Anguished wails rent the air as the poor woman tore off most of her clothes and wept as if her heart was breaking.

Moji blew up a storm over her husband's death but as with all storms, passions were soon spent and the serious business of planning a "befitting burial" was soon taken in hand. Being only a wife, Moji was of course not consulted about how her husband was to be buried. It was simply not her business. The only role due to her was to show up at the funeral.

According to tradition, only those members of the family who were younger than Tolu could be directly involved in getting Tolu properly buried. Because he was so young, there could be no delay in burying the body. Emissaries were immediately sent to the ancestral home, two hundred and fifty kilometres away from Lagos. They were to take the sad news of death to the people at home and to inform them that the body was to be buried in Lagos. The decision to bury Tolu's body in Lagos was hotly contested by some members of the family on the spot. But the points that settled the argument in favour of a burial in Lagos were that, Tolu's mother was still alive and taking his body home to her might be too traumatic for her to cope with. Also, since the funeral was to be immediate, not many of his friends and acquaintances in Lagos would be able to make the journey up-country to give the departed, the last respects which he so richly deserved.

*   *   *   *   *

A little over eight weeks before Tolu died, another death had occurred that was going to bind two families together in a way that was not just unexpected but highly undesirable. Although Chief Ologbenla had died suddenly, his death was not shocking or unexpected for the simple reason that at over eighty years, he had accomplished all that he had in him to accomplish. He himself had waited with impressive equanimity for the great journey, as he called it, long before the fateful event. A few years before, the chief had been diagnosed as being hypertensive. He had been placed on some drugs and advised to keep to a strict diet and avoid alcohol. He was not impressed by the gravity, with which the young doctor, a very pretty lady who looked decidedly out of place in a consulting room, told him that he needed to be careful about his health. The old man had other things on his mind, all of them in the dim past when as a young and not so young man, he had partaken of more than what should have been regarded as his fair share of the pleasures of the flesh.

'Look at this pretty young thing giving me orders as if she knew anything about life' he mused. 'In my heydays, I bet I would have had a great deal to say and do to a fine specimen like this. She certainly looks good enough not to have any problems finding a decent man or even men but, the way young men are these days, one can never be too sure that they are keeping her satisfied. Still, I expect that she has enough to do with herself and may have little left over for men' he concluded on a sympathetic note.

From very far away, Chief Ologbenla heard the doctor give some further instructions, this time about how to take the drugs that had been prescribed for him.

'You will be given two different kinds of tablets, one pink and the other white' he was told in a careful tone. 'The pink one, you must take twice daily, one in the morning and the other one at night, just before you go to bed. As for the white tablets, you will take two of them with your lunch every day. Make sure that you eat well before you take the tablets, which you must wash down with plenty of water. You must on no account take any alcohol and you have to cut down drastically on starchy foods and red meat. On second thoughts, I think you should avoid red meat altogether and take only chicken and fish.'

'Can you repeat what you said about starchy foods?' asked Chief Ologbenla.

'Certainly' replied the doctor. 'You must not indulge yourself with starchy foods such as *eba, iyan* and *amala*. Take beans, a little rice, plenty of vegetables and remember to take plenty of water throughout the day. And whatever you eat, avoid salt. You may find this difficult at first, but never mind, you will soon get used to it.'

'What is this treatment supposed to achieve?' the old man wanted to know.

The young lady who did not have a single humorous bone in her body took the question by its literal meaning.

'This treatment is the very latest in the control of hypertension. In another few weeks, you will be a new man and your chances of staying alive for many, or at least several years will be greatly enhanced.'

'You want to keep me alive for what? I will be alive, at least you think I will be alive, but I will not be able to eat meat or *iyan*. Do you call that being really alive?'

'Well, you cannot eat *iyan* or drink beer, so what? You will be alive!' burst out the doctor who had still not come to the realisation that she was having her shapely legs pulled. The chief may be well past it, but he had always enjoyed feminine company, and age, which may have dulled his appetite for some other things, had not killed off this propensity. He was enjoying his time with the young lady and all he was doing was putting off the inevitable, the time when he would have to take himself off.

'By the way, I hear that some of your tablets can impair a man's performance. You are not giving me one of those, are you?'

The twinkle in his eyes was unmistakable, even for the very serious doctor and she knew at last that her patient was only really enjoying himself at her expense. But she did not mind. The man was good at what he was doing that she felt constrained to reward him with a dazzling smile, one pulled out of the very top drawer.

'Baba!' she responded, stressing the title in such a way that the old man knew the game was up. 'Just do as you are told and everything will be fine. Come back and see me as soon as you have taken all the tablets and I will take another look at you' she promised with another dimpled smile.

To his credit, the chief tried very hard to do as he was told, but his will to stay alive was not as strong as it used to be. Besides, he really did enjoy his *iyan*, his daily bottle of cold beer and as for meat, he preferred it to be red, the redder the better. If these indulgences were to kill him, he had no regrets and so, he carried on pretty much as he always did. He took his drugs as prescribed within the first six months after which he stopped and was not so religious in his observances of other conditions. Long after that, and to his surprise, death refused to come for him.

All throughout this time however, nature was taking its inexorable course. His arteries, which had progressively lost their tone, became narrower and as they narrowed, they offered increasing resistance to blood flow through them so that the pressure with which the heart pumped blood through them also increased. Because the blood vessels had become quite brittle, their ability to withstand this pressure was also reduced and on that fateful day, just after supper, one of the vessels in the brain burst under the strain and flooded that delicate organ with blood. Pressure was very quickly built up within the cranium and the old man collapsed having suffered what in layman's language is a stroke, what the doctors in their incomprehensible dialect call a cardiovascular cerebral accident. Never mind any of the terms, the upshot was that the chief went into a coma and died on the way to the hospital.

Not only was the chief very old, he was a traditional chief and father to no less than seventeen children. Three of them were economic refugees in the USA, two others were in Germany, another one in Russia and several others scattered all over Nigeria. His funeral was going to take some planning -- all of nine hectic weeks.

First, the news of Baba's death was sent to all the relatives in far-flung places. They all dropped whatever it was they were doing and hurried back to attend the funeral. Each of them knew that there was no way the chief could be buried in a hurry but nobody was willing to take any chances. Besides, they all wanted to be present at the meeting at which the funeral plans were to be discussed and levies imposed. Nobody was worried about the will, at least just yet, but they knew that those who were absent were invariably going to be overtaxed. So, they all came immediately. Even the young man who was at that time trying to get an engineering degree from a university in one of the more remote corners of Russia got the call and responded immediately.

Baba had died after a long and fruitful life and although there were some tears, only a few people, and only those who were even older than he was could be said to be bowed with grief. For the most part, it was taken as a gigantic family reunion. This even more than a wedding was regarded as an opportunity to meet, swap stories, renew old acquaintances and exchange gossip until when another one of the family greybeards presented them with another opportunity for the next round of jollities by dying.

Unlike what obtained in many large families, the Ologbenla family was remarkably free of deep-seated antagonisms and so it was not too difficult to agree on what was to be done. The most contentious issue concerned the date and the difficulties arose here principally because of the need to satisfy several competing demands. The chief was a traditional title-holder and so the Oba of his hometown was to be very much involved in the ceremonies. He was a very visible member of the church at home and in Lagos. This being so, the possibility of burying him without two or even more Bishops in attendance could not even be contemplated. Given their heavy schedule of activities, getting one Bishop to be present at any particular event was clearly going to be hellishly difficult but, to get two to agree to the same date was more than doubly so. A lot of deft juggling was called for and all the principals felt that they had accomplished a great deal when it was finally possible for a suitable date -- a little more than nine weeks after the old man died was finally set for the funeral.

The date chosen was a Saturday but for a whole week before, there was no single day when there was no activity connected with the funeral. The members of Baba's church and secular societies, many of whom were too old to undergo the rigours of an 800-kilometre round trip for the funeral were lavishly feasted after the church service on the Sunday before the burial. From Monday through Thursday, services of songs at which inordinately large quantities of sandwiches, *akara* and sundry beverages were consumed were held in the residence of the deceased. A huge wake was organised for the Friday night before the interment in Baba's family compound in his hometown.

The body appropriately washed and decked out in expensive clothes was to be collected from the mortuary and taken up-country on Friday morning. One of Baba's numerous nephews was in charge of this detail and for one full week before the event, the young man had dashed around like one possessed to see that all would be ready for the great day. He did not even forget to tip the mortuary attendants in advance, just to be sure that there would be no hitch.

The chief was to be buried on Saturday afternoon, after which there was to be a party which was to go on all night. All comers were expected so, no' less than fifteen fat cows had been slaughtered to provide meat of the reddest variety for the occasion and there was going to be enough alcohol in many different forms to float a decent battleship. The chief's funeral was billed to be a great celebration of life.

*   *   *   *   *

In sharp contrast to the elaborate preparations for the chief's funeral, Tolu was going to be buried with as little fuss as possible. Apart from buying a decent coffin and paying for the required plot of burial ground, expenses were going to be minimal. There were plans to feed some people, especially those who had come a long way to pay their last respects and even these people were not expected to consume more than what was required to stitch body and soul together.

The funeral plans may not have been elaborate, but there were many things to do all the same. Some ladies had the job of seeing to it that the children were looked after and got ready for the funeral service in good time. Others were to make sure that the guests from out of town were properly accommodated and fed whilst at least two of Moji's closest friends were required to wait on her, giving her physical, mental and spiritual support at every point in time. She had wept herself to the point of insensibility but became more and more agitated as the time for the funeral drew closer. A car was put at her disposal and it was to take her and the children, first to the mortuary where they were to pay their respects and gaze on their father's pallid features for the last time and then to the church. Since nobody could predict the state of Lagos' chaotic traffic situation, it was agreed that they would leave home a long time before the service was due to start. This is why they arrived at the mortuary some one-hour and a half before the scheduled start of the funeral service.

The young man who had the responsibility of seeing to it that Tolu's body was brought to the church was no less conscientious than Chief Ologbenla's nephew who was to perform a similar service for his uncle. He too had taken great care to cross all palms that needed to be crossed with crisp currency notes and he was confident that he would be able to get the body out, well on time. Still, he was not going to take any chances, so he made sure that the hearse and coffin got to the mortuary well before time. Indeed, the conveyance was at the mortuary long before Moji's high-pitched wails announced that she had come to collect her late husband's body.

The day of the funeral had dawned grey and cloudy to match the sombreness of the occasion. It was as if nature itself was in deep mourning. By the early afternoon, the skies began to weep, dropping fat tears, which threatened to drown the ceremony. All around the mortuary, Tolu's relatives and friends who had come to view the body stood in tight little knots, sheltering, or rather, trying to shelter under the few umbrellas that were available. In the meantime, the coffin gleamed in the hearse, waiting to swallow the corpse.

The people had been waiting patiently for a little over half an hour and yet there was no sign that the body was ready to be transferred into the coffin. At that point, there was still plenty of time and so there was little anxiety about getting the body to the church on time. As waiting time crept close to one hour however, people began to wonder what the waiting was all about.

'Have you people done all that should be done?' one of Tolu's uncles who was there in defiance of tradition wanted to know. 'I warned that these young people were sure to bungle things up one way or the other, but nobody would listen to me' grumbled the old man.

This did not produce the body.

Another fifteen minutes went by. Still, no body. By this time Tolu's uncle had become visibly worried. He called over the young man supposedly in charge.

'What is happening here?' he asked, his strangled voice betraying the grievous depth of his emotions.

'Well sir, I don't really know, but I guess they are having a bit of trouble. They have promised to straighten the matter out in another few minutes.'

'Trouble! What kind of trouble can they be having? Tolu's body was brought here. I know that because I saw his name in their register. There is no way the body would have walked out of here so all they have to do is wash it, dress it and put it inside that coffin over there. Don't talk to me about trouble. Just tell them to produce the body, now!'

'Yes sir, I will talk to them' replied the poor fellow, backing away hastily from his irate uncle. He went up to the man in charge of the mortuary and asked him what the matter was.

'We have a little problem' replied the man.

'Problem! What kind of problem can you have?' the young man asked, unconsciously echoing his uncle.

'Well, you see' replied the mortuary attendant scratching his head, to which a few strands of hair were attached here and there, 'the body seems to be missing.'

'Missing! Missing? Did I hear you say that the body we have come to collect is missing?'

'Er, that is right. We cannot find the body.'

The young man turned on his heel abruptly and went up to his elderly relative, the uncle who had been expressing his anxieties very forcefully. Without any preamble, he passed on the information, which he had just been given.

'You can't be serious!' shouted the man. 'Now I know that this country has gone to the dogs. Look, they must be joking, or they are trying to get us to give them more money. Take them out to that hearse so that they can see the quality of the coffin we have brought with us! Make them see that we are people of substance and that they do not have to stoop to mean tricks to get money from us' the man fumed, digging out a very fat purse to show that he meant what he said.

Toye, the young man in charge went off to have another chat with the mortuary attendant and reminded him that he, Toye, had personally paid up all charges, official and otherwise so there was no reason why the body should not have been released to them.

'This is not a matter of money sir', replied the mortuary attendant suddenly discovering a hitherto unsuspected vein of submissiveness.

'Believe me sir, we really cannot find the body. I left instructions concerning it before I left here yesterday and right now, nobody can explain what has happened.'

Toye was stunned. He had been coping well up till that point, but this was too heavy for him to handle. It may be extreme to say that he was struck dumb, but he certainly was not able to utter a single word. He just hung there in utter disbelief.

By this time, there was a large crowd at the mortuary. Those who had come with Moji and the children had been joined by some of the people who had gone straight to the church. The time for the service to start was long past and they had come to find out the cause of the delay. As soon as the women learnt that Tolu's body was missing, they broke into a frenzy, rending their clothes, shouting incoherently and sobbing hard enough to trouble the dead. The reaction of the men was more restrained, but only just. A group of them stormed into the mortuary grimly determined to pull the place apart in search of the body, which had been declared missing.

What they found was as shocking as it was nauseating. The mortuary was built to accommodate eighty bodies at full stretch, but very close to two hundred corpses had been squeezed into it. There were simply bodies everywhere, all of them packed like low-priced goods in a miser's shop. It was apparent that some attempt had been made to establish some order in the place as many of the corpses had nametags attached to them, usually to the big toe of the right foot. One of the more assiduous searchers was horrified to find that many of the tags were obviously wrongly attached, giving up in despair when he found a tag testifying to the fact that the body to which it was attached was a baby. It was in fact attached to the body of a corpulent old man, who would need a coffin measuring a shade over the proverbial six feet whenever his relatives decided to bury him. Searched as they did, Tolu's body was not found. It had no doubt been taken away, hopefully for burial, but more believably, for some unfathomable and sinister purpose.

It was getting dark before the grieving family accepted that Tolu's body was no longer in the mortuary. The people still waiting in the church were duly informed and somebody was sent to the cemetery to tell those who were there that the funeral had been unavoidably postponed indefinitely.

There was nothing for the people to do but go home as best as they could. Before dispersing however there was a great deal of discussion about what could have happened to the body and what could be done to repair the situation. One large and rather vociferous group headed inevitably by Tolu's furious uncle was for calling in the police immediately. They had somehow come to the conclusion that the body had been sold to dealers in human (spare) parts. The hearers of this outrageous suggestion were aghast and some of them argued that it was just not possible that people traded in such grisly wares. One of the supporters of this suggestion was outraged that his position could be doubted.

'Some of you people know nothing about what is going on all around you. I didn't think that I could come across an adult in Lagos who does not know that people deal in human parts. Why, you can get any part you want from some popular markets in Lagos. All you need is plenty of money and you can make your choice.'

'And what would anyone want to do with human parts?' asked an obviously bewildered man who was visibly upset by the situation in which they were in and the possibility that his poor friend's body may, even as they spoke, be in the process of being dismembered.

'You have no idea what people can do to get money. The answer to your question is simple. Human parts are the vital ingredients in charms, which are used in making money. And for your information, there are people who are specialists in the preparation of such charms.'

'How did you come to know about these things?' the man was asked.

'By keeping my ears and eyes wide open' he retorted.

'You must not dismiss these things' another man warned. 'Only last year, there was a curious incident in a house near where I live. Two women were quarrelling over whose turn it was to clean their communal kitchen and as you know with women, one thing led to another and they started revealing all the secrets, which they had unwisely entrusted to each other over the years. You can imagine the stir that was created when one of them accused the other of resorting to the use of charms to entice people into her shop. She then went on to inform her shocked listeners that she was present when her current antagonist paid for, and took delivery of a forefinger removed from a recently dead man. The finger, together with some other less exotic items was put into a little round tin and buried in the other woman's shop. We all trooped to the shop and within a few minutes, discovered the gruesome exhibit.'

'What happened to the woman?' asked a man who had become caught up with the story and was determined to have his curiosity about it satisfied. He was more than slightly disappointed when the raconteur replied in weary tones: 'The two women were taken to the police-station but nothing came of it. Having "settled" the police, they were both released shortly afterwards, and what more, the two women patched up their quarrel and are now friends again.'

By that time, it had become quite dark and the people began to disperse most of them to look for something to eat and a willing ear to pour the day's experience into. Some of them from out of town were also faced with the problem of finding suitable accommodation at short notice and they turned their minds to the satisfaction of this end.

The members of Tolu's extended family in Lagos did not give any thought to food or shelter. They were too shaken to remember anything about physical desires. Although no prior decision had been taken to that effect, they all retired to the home of their oldest relative, Chief Adejare to deliberate on how an appropriate response to this inexplicable calamity could be fashioned. It was simply too awful that they could not find the body of their kinsman for burial. At that point they had stopped worrying about whether they had prepared a decent funeral for Tolu, or not. They would have been happy to bury the body any way they could, if only they could find it.

The scene in Chief Adejare's house to where the family retired was chaotic to say the least. People were everywhere, talking passionately about the missing body and the dark omen, which it portended. Every now and then, one of the women raised her voice in loud lamentation and the others responded with louder wails so that the place rang with heart-rending noise. The men were crammed into their host's sitting-room and there, reviewed the situation in an attempt to formulate a plan to pull out their chestnuts from the raging fire, a fire so fierce that it could consume not only the chestnuts, but they, the tenders as well. It was a grave assembly.

Chief Adejare started them off with a long and sonorous prayer. He prayed for the soul of the 'faithful departed', his wife and immediate family before taking the Good Lord to task about allowing the terrible thing that had happened, especially to people of God. After conceding that all power belonged to God who could not be questioned about anything, he next pleaded for divine guidance so that they, puny mortals that they were, could solve this problem to the glory of the Most High. The Amen at the end of it was thunderous.

This meeting, given the sole item on the agenda was always going to be emotional and it would have taken the skill and diligence of an experienced team of chroniclers to prepare an accurate account of it. Even then, unless the account was subjected to extensive editorial amendments, it would have been incomprehensible to all but the most astute readers. The highlights of this imaginary document would have been that "the house decided to reject the suggestion that Tolu's body had been smuggled out of the mortuary by people with sinister motives. Rather, it was decided that a mistake had been made and that all efforts to rectify the situation must be made immediately. It was the general belief that Tolu's body had been released to another family by mistake." Those of them who had seen the chaotic situation in the mortuary at first-hand defended this position very stoutly and in the end, succeeded in convincing the others that the starting point for the investigation must be the mortuary.

The meeting broke up close to midnight but the lateness of the hour did not discourage action. Three of the younger members of the family were sent off to the mortuary to try and get as much information as they could so that any leads could be followed up before the trail went cold.

By the nature of work done within them, mortuaries are, even in the dead of night never dead, so that when the investigators arrived at the mortuary, they found a couple of attendants trying desperately to keep awake. As soon as the nocturnal visitors explained their mission, all traces of sleep were instantly wiped from the attendants' visage. Wiped away as if by magic. They had been told about the drama, which had unfolded earlier in the day and were very anxious to defend the honour of their establishment. They knew that the disappearance of bodies from mortuaries fell well within the province of a man biting a dog, an event, which invariably attracted journalists of the investigative kind. They recognised the need for damage limitation and appreciated that the most important means of preventing their establishment from being savaged in the press was to show every courtesy to the aggrieved party. Gone into cold storage at it were, was the abrasive face which they usually presented to the grieving and helpless public.

'We will do our best to be of help to you, sir' the older of the two attendants assured their visitors.

'How many bodies were released for burial today?' asked Sope, the leader of the investigating group.

The attendant brought out a bulky and well-thumbed ledger, opened it to the relevant page and with a gnarled finger, went down the most recent entries and gave out the information that the day being Saturday, no less than seven bodies had been collected.

'Does that book contain information about bodies released?' asked another member of the team.

'Yes, yes' the attendant assured his audience.

'What can you tell us about the bodies?'

'I can give you the name, age, sex, date of demise, the name of the person who collected the body and his contact address,' came the prompt response.

'In that case, what can you tell us about the bodies, which were collected today?'

'Well, I see that four of the bodies were female, two were juvenile males who were brought in earlier in the day. The other body was also brought in this morning but being Muslim. it was taken out again almost immediately.'

'Hmm' responded Sope; 'none of those could have been mistaken for Tolu, so let us see what we have for Friday.'

The book was duly consulted and the information was given that two bodies had been collected the day before. Both were male. One was to be buried right there in Lagos and the other, that of one Chief Ologbenla was to be buried in some village in Ondo State. Both were promising leads, which the team decided were worth following up. They asked questions about the bodies that had been collected since Tolu's body was brought in. In the end, it was decided that if a mistake had been made it would have to be in connection with one of the bodies, which had been collected the day before Tolu's scheduled funeral.

After coming to this decision, the investigators decided to call it a day, but also decided to reconvene early the next day to follow up on what they had found out so far. On his way home, the leader of the team stopped by in Chief Adejare's house to take further instructions. Chief Adejare who could not even think of sleep was in his sitting-room, keeping pointless vigil with almost a score of people who were afflicted with the same condition of sleeplessness.

Chief Adejare if not actually pleased with the information which was brought to him, was at least satisfied that some progress had been made. His instruction was that the team should make an early morning visit to the address in Lagos where one of the bodies had been taken and if necessary to set out on the long journey to Ondo State. Given all these however, they were dimly aware that these were actions of despair because it was unlikely that a man could be buried without his relatives, grieving or not, making sure of the identity of the body being put away. Still, there could be no harm in trying.

The first leg of the investigation was over very quickly the next day. They found the area around the address they wanted, liberally littered with the debris of a huge all-night party. There were not many people around and those who were available were clearly exhausted. They were however conscious enough to assure their strange and uninvited guests that their dear departed was laid out in state for nearly three hours before the coffin was finally closed and sealed. There could be no doubt whatsoever about which body was buried the day before. They buried the right body all right!

*   *   *   *   *

The arrangements for Chief Ologbenla's burial were so elaborate that it could be expected that something would go wrong. Most ceremonies have to go on regardless of hitches and so the family did not expect that everything would come out exactly right on the day.

At the crack of dawn on the Friday before the funeral, the members of the family in Lagos and their friends started shipping out so that they could make adequate preparations for the main body of invitees who were expected to arrive that evening or early on Saturday.

The nephew who was to ship the body home had taken the robes in which the corpse was to be decked out on the day before so that it could be dressed early on Friday morning. He had planned to come out to the mortuary at the crack of dawn to supervise the operation, but his plans went awry and he arrived all of four hours behind schedule. He had been unlucky enough to run foul of the notorious Lagos traffic. It was certainly not his fault that a huge truck hauling a long trailer had jack-knifed blocking one of the main roads through the city and causing traffic to build up on both sides of the blockage. The situation was made intractable by the impatience of the first drivers to arrive on the scene. All of them wanted to find a way around the blockage but instead of doing that, they simply made matters worse and very quickly, the road not only became impassable but sent the effects of the blockage all over the city.

As the traffic build-up got worse, the chief's nephew got more desperate but there was nothing he could do about it. A journey that should have taken no more than half an hour was stretched to just under five agonising hours and by the time the poor man arrived at the mortuary, the body had already been coffined and they were set to roll. They had to find their way out of Lagos through little known back streets where they got lost on two occasions. They were therefore hopelessly behind schedule, but their misfortune was not yet over as the hearse had a breakdown on the Lagos-Ibadan expressway. They were delayed for another hour or so. By this time, the poor man was fuming with impatience and he urged the man driving the hearse to go faster so that the body could be brought home to meet at least part of the wake.

In the meantime, the people at the other end were getting worried. But since Lagos was by no stretch of the imagination just down the road, they felt that there may have been a delay somewhere and that whatever happened, the corpse would be brought in before the wake was due to begin. But the people were not reassured by their own contrived excuses and wanted the body to arrive so that the festivities could begin.

By the time it got dark, there was nobody left who was not worried, most of them deeply so. Even the Oba who by tradition was not expected to be physically present at the funeral had become very anxious. The chief's body could not be brought into the town until after the Oba had been informed through the performance of certain rituals which were the medium through which the Oba was officially informed that one of his chiefs had died. Following this, the Oba was expected to give the family leave to bury the body. This was indeed why the Oba had to be consulted before a date was fixed for the funeral. And so, from the Oba to the humblest of his subjects, everybody in the town was on tenterhooks. When night fell and the body had not arrived, the elders of the family held a hasty meeting and decided that the wake should begin. Their wishes were complied with, but even as they sang they kept one ear open for the sound of the convoy accompanying the hearse.

The service was in full swing when a vehicle being driven at high speed was stopped noisily in front of Chief Ologbenla's house. The people, thinking they were now going to be given news of what had held up the convoy bringing Baba home focused their attention on the new arrivals. Everybody was eager to hear what he or she had to say, but there was some intangible but potent force around them, which made it impossible for anybody to approach them directly. The two men ignored everybody pointedly and walked up to one of the priests conducting the service and had a brief, whispered conversation with him. The gist of the message, which they passed on to him, was that there had been an accident, the aftermath of which was that the body they were bringing in for burial was lost.

Nobody was interested in the detailed description of what had happened, possibly because nobody could supply such details. It was such a simple and straightforward occurrence. Six kilometres from the town on the Lagos side, was a narrow bridge across a small, deep and swift river. This river provided the town with fish, but it was also so treacherous that it had lured many people into its depths over the years and therefore only approached with extreme caution. It was indeed only approached because of the rich harvest of fishes, which it yielded up regularly time after time.

The town is not situated on a major road and the bridge, which was thrown across the notorious bridge by the long-departed colonial authorities, was rather narrow and not designed to carry much traffic. It was however carefully maintained until after the country's independence when it became the victim of bureaucratic amnesia so that even the sign, which warned of the presence of a "narrow bridge ahead" was allowed to fade and subsequently to collapse. There was of course no thought of any replacement. How could there be when even the railings on the bridge were in course of time removed by people who reasoned that they were not serving any useful purpose on the bridge and found that they could find other, very private uses for them. The bridge was therefore just a long slab of concrete, which spanned the river.

The indigenes of the town and frequent travellers in those parts were well aware of the existence of that bridge and began to look out for it long before it came into view at the end of a rather sharp bend. For many travellers, the bridge was not even seen and many journeys came to a watery end right there. The spot became quite notorious, even legendary. In a place where fantasy, the more lurid, the better is consistently more believable than proven facts, the cause of the many accidents that occurred with alarming regularity on that bridge was ascribed to the malevolent spirit of the river. Many elaborate sacrifices were performed there, to no purpose as the accidents continued to happen, no less frequently than before.

The hearse bringing Chief Ologbenla's body home was driven by a first-time visitor to the area. He had no idea of the danger ahead and in any case, was trying to make up for part of the time lost by going a little faster than safety demanded on that narrow road. He was just straightening out of what he thought was a normal curve in the road when the bridge sprang up in front of him like the product of a conjurer's trick. He was going too fast to control his vehicle as he needed to, and this maneuver was made more difficult by the gathering gloom by which the place was surrounded. He lost control of the vehicle, smashed into a pillar, which had quite miraculously survived many such shattering encounters and took a long dive into the dark waters of the river. The coffin, jolted by the impact, broke loose and came flying out of the back of the hearse with the velocity of a shell exploding out of the muzzle of a howitzer and landed in the water with an almighty splash. The driver was trapped in his cab and the first consideration of the people in the accompanying vehicles was to free him and his passenger, the chief's nephew as quickly as they could. This is why nobody took any notice of the coffin, which landed a fair distance from the point at which the hearse went into the river. The coffin first bobbed gently on the surface of the river as if testing its watery environment before it started moving away with the current which was not very strong at that point. It soon began to pick up speed however as it got near a small cataract and when it hit that point in the river, it began to travel quite fast. Before anyone was properly awake to the possibility of the coffin floating away downstream, it was gone. Gone forever.

A large crowd of people had gathered in town for the chief's funeral and when they learnt about what had happened, they put their hands on their heads and wept unrestrainedly. The funeral as planned, was to be a joyous occasion, a rousing send-off to a man who, by the standards of the day was a success and an inspiration. Now, they were in deep mourning, not because their man was dead, but because, as they saw it, the very soil of his native town had rejected his body. Everyone knew the process by which the body was lost. It was as clear as day that an accident had been responsible. There could be no arguing with that. The mystery which needed to be answered was why it was the hearse bringing the body home and not any other vehicle that was involved in that particular accident. As far as they were concerned, nothing happened by chance. There was a reason why that accident had occurred and it was this reason that they wanted to find out.

There was a great deal of speculation regarding the accident and although there were many shades of opinion, a good student of the situation would have discovered that there were two broad schools of thought on this matter.

Some of the people were more or less convinced that the villain of the peace in this matter was the river spirit, at the height of its spitefulness. As far as the protagonists of this position were concerned, the spirit should have been appeased with the appropriate sacrifices before the child's body was brought home. In other words, the organisers of the funeral should have formally informed the spirit of the river of their intentions and reverently asked for permission to carry on with their planned programme. The organisers should have known that the spirit would have been irritated by all the attention being paid to a mere man. Chief Ologbenla may have been an outstanding personality, but to elevate him above "spiritual powers" was to court disaster.

The other school of thought took a diametrically opposite view. According to them, the river in this instance was only an agent acting on behalf of the earth, which for one reason or the other did not want the chief to be buried in her. If this was the case, and they were sure it was, then there was much about the chief that they did not know. After all, the earth rejected only those that had committed some particularly heinous crime or crimes.

Although more of the people were inclined to be in the first (river) group, there were enough people in the earth group for the issue to become truly bipartisan. The arguments boiled over furiously throughout the day on which the chief was to have been buried and generated so much excitement that there were a few scuffles all over town. The Oba had sent out his chiefs with instructions to see that peace was maintained. Fortunately, the news that there was no body to be buried had not spread far and wide and so, most of the visitors who were being expected duly turned up and, funeral or no funeral had to be fed. The singing and dancing portions of the programme had to be shelved but a lot of food was consumed, the peculiar circumstance notwithstanding.

Mid-morning on Sunday and the whole town was still buzzing with the drama of the lost body when a car entered the town from the Lagos end. Its passengers were obviously strangers because they had to ask the way to Chief Ologbenla's house, a piece of intelligence that was at the fingertips of every man, woman and most children in the town. The people thought that the visitors were stragglers who had been invited to the funeral, but who had not been able to come the day before. A young man who had come down from Ibadan for the funeral gave them directions.

The new comers were none other than those who had been sent down from Lagos by Chief Adejare to make inquiries about Tolu's corpse. There were three men and one woman in the team which was led by one of the older members of the family who at nearly seventy years of age was thought to have the requisite experience to deal with what was clearly a very tricky situation. It was recognised that young men could be very useful when heavy objects were to be shifted, but when grey matter was in demand, greybeards were infinitely preferable.

The leader of the team was Baba to the others and it was he that did all the talking when they arrived at their destination.

The first thing to be got out of the way was the greeting, which was very formal. All the elders of the Ologbenla family were present and each one of them was greeted respectfully. Nobody appeared to be in any hurry to do anything and Baba himself was the very picture of patience. Condolences were graciously offered and received no less graciously. It was only when all protocol had been duly observed that the subject of the visit was broached.

'We have come to try and solve the riddle of a missing body' began Baba tentatively. He failed at this point to notice the startled glances, which his hosts threw at him.

'Hmm!' was the most eloquent verbal response that he got, so he had to try a new tack.

'We need your help' he went on 'and we would be grateful for any help, which you can give us over this delicate matter. We need to ask a few questions about the body, which you buried yesterday.'

At this point, his hearers were staring at him open-mouthed.

'But, we did not bury any body yesterday. You see, there was nothing to bury as the coffin fell into the river and was carried off by the current!'

Now it was the turn of the visitors to lose control of the mechanism that was normally responsible for keeping their mouths shut.

'You mean you lost a body too!' exclaimed Baba after a decent interval during which he struggled to pull himself together. He then told them how they got to the mortuary and found that the body they had gone to collect was missing.

'We came here hoping that the corpse that you were supposed to have buried yesterday was the body we wanted to inter and that you would have discovered that you had the wrong body.'

'In that case, there is little we can do for you because none of us talking to you now actually saw the body' the visitors were informed.

'What about those who went to collect the body? Surely, they took a look at it. We just want to be absolutely certain that no mistake had been made in the matter of identification.'

This was when the nephew who had been in charge of bringing the body was sent for. He had been involved in the accident that claimed his uncle's body and although he had been lucky to come away with only a few bruises, he was still much shaken by that experience. He went through the elaborate process of greeting everyone present and was waved to a chair into which he sank very stiffly due to his inability to bend those of his joints, which had been affected by the accident. He was soon stiff with embarrassment when he was asked about the identity of the corpse that he was bringing home for burial.

'Did you make sure that it was your uncle's body in that coffin?' asked the oldest man present.

The poor fellow, instead of providing an answer, looked all around him in confusion.

'Did you see the body at any point before the coffin was closed?' he was then asked.

'Er, no' he blurted out at last.

He then went on to tell them in great detail how he got caught up in a mammoth traffic jam. And how he was consequently so far behind schedule that he simply took delivery of the loaded coffin and tried to get it home as quickly as he could, bearing in mind that all the roads around the hospital were still blocked.

'Do you mean that there is no way of ascertaining whose body was in that coffin?' the leader of the visiting delegation asked him excitedly.

'No, there is none. Unless the driver of the hearse got a good look at the body. It did not occur to me in the rush that a mistake could have been made or that there was even a remote possibility that it was not my uncle's body in that coffin.'

Since no stone was to be left unturned in the course of this investigation, the poor driver who was hardly out of shock was dragged out of bed and subjected to questioning. As he had never set eyes on the late chief however, his testimony was not regarded as very reliable and indeed he was not of very much help. After all he did not look at the body with the objective of establishing the identity of the corpse. Yes, he took a look at the body, but he thought the body was that of an old man. After a whispered conversation, the Lagos delegation decided that this information was hardly useful given the fact that Tolu, when he died could have been described as being very old by those who had known him all his life, not to talk of a casual acquaintance.

'This situation has to be handled very carefully' Baba said ponderously and totally unnecessarily as nobody was thinking of doing anything in any way other than carefully, very carefully.

In the end however, the matter was resolved quickly. The only thing to do in the circumstance was to go back to the mortuary to find if the chief's body was still there. The earlier this was done the better and so the two families set out for Lagos straightaway. The journey back to Lagos was a tense one. Chief Ologbenla's people were hoping that they would have a second chance at staging a high profile funeral. The other party did not know what to hope for. If Chief Ologbenla's body was still in the mortuary, then it would be assumed that the body which was washed away was Tolu's, but since there was no way of confirming this, the doubts would never be removed. If on the other hand, the chief's body was no longer in the mortuary, then their search had to continue.

All the people involved in this bizarre saga of missing corpses had high hopes that their dilemma would be resolved one way or the other. Each side prayed fervently that the issue be resolved in their own favour. Both parties refused to countenance the possibility that neither side would find satisfaction. They drove straight to the mortuary and for the second time in twenty-four hours, a powerful ray of light was beamed into the murky nooks and crannies of that most sedate of institutions and for the second time within the same period, the searchers were not rewarded with success. After a freezing hour, it was agreed that neither Chief Ologbenla's nor Tolu's body was still lodged in the mortuary. Neither party had been satisfied but the Ologbenla party went home, the seeds of doubt buried in a fertile corner of their imagination.

They could not help asking: whose body was it that was swallowed up by the dark waters of that cursed river?

Andrew Checks Out

The year 1985 was a turning point in many lives. The 30 million Nigerians who were reputed to be addicted to NTA's nightly news broadcasts were told the story of Andrew as daily food for thought. To those who were away on Mars or somewhere else almost equally inaccessible and so never made Andrew's acquaintance, this gentleman was a rather pudgy Nigerian with a phony American accent who out of frustration was "checking out", this being the phrase for describing the process of fleeing the country. According to Andrew, he had become thoroughly fed up with all the irritations, major and minor, but mostly major which were characteristic of life in Nigeria at that time. He was therefore going off to the glorious US of A where he could fulfil himself and lead, as much as possible, what could be described as a normal life.

Andrew was on the verge of boarding his plane when some busybody, full of the spirit of WAI (War Against Indiscpline) and spurious patriotism dissuaded him from checking out. The rulers of Nigeria at that time declared a bitter war against the indiscpline, which they saw as a great stumbling block to societal progress. One component of this war was a spirited attempt to create a patriotic awareness in the country. It was at that time that all government institutions as part of WAI were forced to fly the national flag. All had to comply with this injunction even if the flag on their masthead was tattered and discoloured. And many of them were! Life may have been very difficult, but WAI forced Nigerians to become suitably patriotic.

Absconding from the country could, in no stretch of the imagination be described as patriotic. Indeed, it was regarded as an act of betrayal, from which any reasonable Nigerian should be dissuaded. In the heady rhetoric of those days, Andrew was told that it was his responsibility as an honest Nigerian to stay in the country, all irritations notwithstanding, and make his own vital contributions to the upliftment of the fatherland. The man from WAI was nothing if not persuasive.

'Look,' he pleaded, 'the country you are going to, was once as poor as Nigeria is today and it is only the hard work and determination of early generations of Americans that has made it possible for that country to be the desired destination of people from all over the world. Had those early Americans checked out of their country as you are doing now, where would their country be today? In any case, you just want to go and reap where you did not sow.'

'There is no chance of my reaping where I did not sow' replied Andrew heatedly. `I am not going to America for any handouts. I am going there to work for every cent that I will spend. I am no less ready to work in this our country, but I am not even allowed to work. There is a lot that I can do, but nobody works in this country for their living, so what am I supposed to do?'

The man from WAI was not discouraged but stuck to his task with admirable fortitude. 'The government is determined to change the face of this country' he cried, his voice ringing with honest conviction. 'Stay home and play your part in the building of a new and strong country. You will be very glad you did. There is no need to bring up your children among strangers when this country is bursting with resources with which we can build a country in which poverty will be a thing of the past. It is Nigerians like you who must work hard, just as earlier generations of Americans worked tirelessly and in many cases, laid down their lives to build the foundation on which the current prosperity of their country rests so comfortably and securely.'

Andrew appeared to have fallen under the spell of the man from WAI because as all NTA viewers will remember, he decided at the very last minute to abandon his plans and to stay in Nigeria to do his own share of salvaging. Now, ten years later, one wonders what became of Andrew and of his efforts to salvage Nigeria from the quicksand into which the country was steadily sinking at the time when checking out appeared to be the only avenue for self-fulfilment. In the cold light of present-day reality, can Andrew look back without regret at his momentous decision to help salvage Nigeria?

Why was Andrew checking out? Nigeria of 1985 was not a comfortable place to live in. The new military government at the time appeared determined to build a new country and was at the height of their not inconsiderable powers. For the first time since the British decorated the country with the symbols of nationhood, Nigerians were being subjected to a massive dose of discipline. Powerful traditional rulers who in earlier times had appeared to be above the laws of the land were brought back to earth with an almighty bump. Two of them who thought that they were even more powerful than other traditional rulers were confined to their palaces for visiting Israel, a country with which Nigeria did not have diplomatic relations.

Currency smugglers were a particular menace at that time. They sold the Naira at ridiculous prices to crooked traders thereby undermining the health of the country's currency. In a surprise attack, all currency notes were withdrawn from circulation and replaced with new ones. The currency touts had their backs broken.

Drug pushing had at that time just become the most lucrative occupation for ambitious Nigerians. People became incredibly wealthy literally overnight by stuffing themselves with heroin or some other narcotic substance and getting them to clients overseas. The government enacted a decree and suddenly drug pushing became a capital offence. To make it even worse, the decree was made retroactive and to everyone's horror, three young men who had the misfortune of having been apprehended long before the decree was promulgated were dragged out of their cells one fine day and executed by firing squad. Drug pushing became instantly unattractive and all those couriers who flaunted their new wealth with disgusting joyous abandon started to slink around in great fear for their lives. Many of them left town, vowing never to return.

Even as this was going on, a spirited attempt was made to squeeze money out of those whom, when they were in the government swallowed public funds and exposed the country to poverty and debt. Even those of them who had fled the country were hunted down, drugged and crated and would have been smuggled back into the country to face trial but for the vigilance of British officials. Debt repayments were being made to our numerous creditors both inside and outside the country; the strength of the Naira was being kept up, albeit at considerable discomfort to most Nigerians, some of who lost their jobs. Even the streets of Lagos were not spared. For the first time in two decades, they were actually clean!

The general situation was terrible, but it was his own personal situation that forced Andrew to take the option of checking out. He had been trained on a federal government scholarship in the USA. Having acquired two fine degrees, he came back home fully convinced that he deserved to live in plush comfort for the rest of his life. He had worked in the States like a slave for a couple of years after his studies and had acquired all the signs and symbols of an affluent lifestyle. He had bought a bulky Volvo for himself and a slim Toyota for his wife. He brought with him all the way from the States, an expensive suite of Swedish furniture, an impressive list of Japanese electrical and electronic gadgets and enough Italian suits to set up a posh men's boutique. He was ready for anything, or so he thought.

Things did not immediately go according to plan for Andrew. After the euphoria of home-coming had died down, he was faced with the intimidating array of problems associated with settling down in Nigeria after a lengthy sojourn abroad. Andrew's first problem was to clear his personal effects through customs.

The day he received notice of the arrival of his goods from the USA was a very happy one for Andrew. Now he could begin to live like a man of means. A man of substance who deserved to be treated with respect. Little did he know that there was an ordeal ahead of him. First, he had to find a reliable clearing agent and he soon found that this was not an easy p̶ ̶ ̶ ̶n. True, clearing agents were thick on the ground, but which of them could be trusted not to clear the goods into his own warehouse? Left to him, he would have picked on the first agent that came his way, but his brother-in-law, who was more worldly-wise than Andrew advised him to take great care in choosing his clearing agent.

When the clearing started, Andrew soon found out that his brother-in-law's advice was invaluable as he came across several overseas clients who had been taken to the cleaners by their sleek and unscrupulous clearing agent. Andrew eventually hitched his fortunes in this respect to those of Goodwill Agencies recommended by one of his friends who gave Goodwill, a sterling testimonial.

Goodwill Agencies performed with a will, but even they could not give adequate protection to Andrew from the army of crooked Customs officials who were hell-bent on fleecing all those who had the misfortune of having to do business with them.

'You have a lot of things to clear, sir and you will have to pay a heavy bribe to the Customs before you can claim your goods' warned Tolu, the young agent handling his business.

'Why would anyone ask me for a bribe when I am not bringing in anything that I shouldn't?' asked the bewildered Andrew.

'This is Nigeria, sir and I can assure you that nobody can take anything out of these ports without paying out to the boys.'

'Boys, which boys?' Andrew wanted to know.

'The Customs boys, sir' replied Tolu.

'You mean that these people make blatant demands for bribes without fear of getting caught and punished?' asked the incredulous Andrew.

'The Customs boys operate at the highest levels, sir and they say that not even the Comptroller of Customs can get anything past his own boys without giving them something however small as a token of his respect for them.'

'Is that so? Well the boys as you call them have a thing coming to them because I am determined not to give them anything.'

'You don't have to give them anything, sir. Part of our charges is for the boys, which is why they are so high. We know that most of you people coming in from abroad have these wild notions and they can only be a hindrance to us, so we simply add the money for bribes to the charges and we save ourselves and many others a headache. We don't relish the prospects of suffering for nothing. I have to warn you however that there is one point at which you have to pay the bribe yourself.'

'Why is that?'

'The man at that point is very unpredictable and there is no way we can guess how much he is going to charge. You see there are ways of calculating how much we have to pay at other points and this makes it easy for us to know exactly how much to add to our own bill.'

'We will see about that' was Andrew's grim promise.

A veteran of the Ports Authority manned the all-important point at which no fixed charges were paid. It was the duty of this man to issue a gate pass to people whose goods had been cleared through Customs. Without this pass, it was of course impossible for anyone to take anything out of the ports. What made that point more important than any other was that as far as the port authorities were concerned, any goods at that point had already passed out of their hands and responsibility. They could therefore not be called to account in case such goods went missing. Goods at that point could be described as being in limbo.

Andrew was determined not to pay anything to the vulpine creature that controlled this gate and he declared his intention in no uncertain manner as soon as the man made his inevitable demand for gratification. The old man, who looked like a man well past the statutory retirement age, ignored him completely after informing him that there was no way that his things would be allowed out of the port unless he paid "something". There were no arguments nor raised voices and anyone looking for an altercation would have been grievously disappointed. But the gate remained resolutely shut. A couple of men going about their own business advised Andrew to pay the man. According to them, he ran the risk of losing everything to the robbers who were always on the lookout for people stranded at that point so that they could take possession of goods, which as far as the authorities were concerned had been passed over to the consignee. At this point, Andrew was forced to open negotiations with the man.

'Look mister, I don't have any money on me and I wouldn't be able to pay you anything, even if I wanted to.'

'There is no way you can be out on the streets of Lagos without having any money on you' was the crushing response. 'In any case, that is no business of mine. I have been at this post for more than twenty years now and in all that time, nobody has got anything past me without paying. And let me tell you, that includes all the important men and women that you have heard about and many more besides. This thing is a matter of principle. I don't care how much you pay me, but pay you must.'

True to the clearing agent's sound prediction, Andrew had to pay "something" before he could get his goods past that Cerberus clone.

Even though the relevant fees, both official and unofficial were paid in full and promptly too, the clearing took an inordinately long time. More unfortunately, the poor man had to contend with the loss of a large suitcase full of the goodies with which he had hoped to dazzle his many friends who had stayed at home. Everyone assured him that he had indeed got off lightly and that he should thank his lucky stars that it was not much worse. He really did not believe that he had been lucky until he met a fellow who told him the sad story of how a whole container load of his personal effects had simply vanished from the ports, never to be seen again.

The troubles associated with getting his things through Customs were just the beginning of a catalogue of horrors for poor Andrew. Although he had come from the USA with rather a lot of money, it was not long before he had to settle down to looking for a suitable job. The prospects of finding a job held no terrors for him since nobody could argue with the certificates, which testified to his not inconsiderable skills as a marketer. The first thing he did was to write a sheaf of letters to many of the largest companies in the land, telling all those who cared to listen that he was available for employment, provided of course that the salary and allowances were attractive enough to tempt him. He put all the letters in the post and confidently expected a corresponding avalanche of mouthwatering offers. He waited in vain. When after three months, it became clear that no response was forthcoming, Andrew began to fret. His dollars were disappearing and more than ever, he needed a job.

In the end, Andrew had to turn to his friends for help in landing a job.

'This is a country in which you can never expect to get something for nothing' he was advised by Sam, another returnee from Stateside.

'What do you mean by not getting something for nothing?' asked the bemused Andrew.

'Ah, my friend, my good friend' laughed Sam. 'Forget about how things are in the good old US of A. Here the only thing that talks is money. If you want a job, you have to find someone important to recommend you to somebody else who needs your services and then you have to pay a great deal of cold cash to your prospective employer. You may even have to give something valuable to the man who introduced you to your employer.'

'But I have very little money and those people you are talking about, are likely to be loaded down with the stuff. It is just not fair!'

'How do you think all those big men got their money? Well, I'll tell you. They are rich because they take money from all and sundry. For many of them no amount of money is too small to be pocketed and as you can imagine, small amounts of money soon build up to make a great fortune. So my friend, you are advised to go and find a benefactor or else you will be an "applicant" for a long time to come.'

In the end, Andrew was luckier than most. He had attended a famous secondary school, or at least it was famous when he was a student there twenty years before. Many of the products of the school were professionals who had very good jobs and it was not too difficult, using the old boy network to find a suitable job for one of their own. It needs not be said that most of his contemporaries did not have the opportunity of this advantage and had to pay through the nose for the privilege of earning a decent salary. As matters stood, Andrew got a very good job without having to pay through the nose for it. Furthermore, the job came with very comfortable accommodation and so he did not have to squat with his cousin in one of the less salubrious areas of Lagos, for more than six months.

Andrew had been materially comfortable in the USA, but at no time had he been psychologically comfortable there and so he revelled in the warm feeling of being treated like a human being once again. After the nearly aseptic municipal cleanliness of a medium-sized American city, Andrew found the sights and smells of Lagos a little too strong at the beginning. As time went on however, the smell of poorly maintained open drains and careless sewage disposal was considered a fair price to pay for not being the subject of cold stares from people. People who did not bother to disguise the fact that they begrudged him the privilege of treading what they jealously regarded as being their very own piece of the earth.

Within a short period of time, Andrew had become adapted to living in the steamy jungle of Lagos. He woke up at the crack of dawn and joined the unending queue of cars and dangerously rickety buses crammed with masses of anxious humanity trying to get to work on the island. He got back home very late everyday, but so did everyone else and indeed, his fellow Lagosians wore their late home-coming as a badge of pride. Andrew was soon boasting as much as any other Lagosian about the monster traffic jams, or go-slows as they called them, which it had been his luck to encounter and trotting this out as his excuse for coming back home long after his children had gone to bed. To tell the truth, his lateness was on a number of occasions due to meetings with certain young ladies whom his wife would not have approved of, but she did not get to know this so all was well. Andrew began to put on weight from lack of exercise, but everyone, (except Andrew) regarded this as an infallible sign of the high life.

Quite without warning, Andrew's life began to come apart at the seams. His firm lost a big contract because the Managing Director did not know whom to bribe so that the firm could lay hands on an import licence and more than half of the work force had to be laid off. Andrew escaped the big drop but had to endure a hefty cut in salary. It was at this time that his precious car was snatched at gunpoint in broad daylight by armed robbers. For weeks after he was robbed, Andrew was still dazed by the surreal quality of that experience. It was a rather quiet Saturday afternoon and Andrew was on the Badagry expressway minding his own business, listening to Diana Ross on the car stereo as he drove along. A car zipping along at dangerous speed suddenly overtook him. Andrew, like any warm-blooded Lagosian was on the verge of hurling abuse at the occupants of the car when he noticed that they had gone far out of the range of his insults and he returned to Diana Ross. But not for long. Only a couple of minutes later, he noticed that the same car had made a U-turn and was now coming at him on the wrong side of the expressway. He would have had a great deal to say to these reckless souls, but he was not given the opportunity to say anything as the men came at him with guns blazing! No further persuasion was necessary to force him to a halt. In the twinkling of an eye, he had been forced out of the driver's seat, but not out of the car. Two of his attackers were in the car with him, one of them was driving and the other had a gun to Andrew's head.

'Please don't kill me' he pleaded in a very small voice as his hijackers sped away. They ignored him pointedly, at least until they had gone the distance of about fifteen kilometres when the maniac at the wheel suddenly applied the brakes throwing Andrew about the car like a rag doll. Before he could register what was really happening, he had been kicked out of his own car and into the gutter by the side of the road. The robbers immediately resumed their reckless progress and drove on out of Andrew's life, forever as it turned out.

Those who heard about this operation assured Andrew that he was lucky to be alive. Many other people had been killed in similar situations. What puzzled the poor man more than anything else about that episode was why the robbers had taken him with them for those few hair-raising minutes. It was explained to him that many car owners had fitted all sorts of anti-theft devices to their cars and one of the most effective allowed the stolen car to be driven a few kilometres before stopping. He had been taken along in case the car's demobiliser needed to be demobilised in which case he would have been forced to do whatever was necessary, before in many cases being demobilised in turn by a well-placed shot. What the smart people were doing at that time was taking out whatever security gadget they had installed in their cars. After all it was infinitely better for one to lose a car than to prevent its theft at the cost of one's life.

Andrew's car had been snatched by professionals. It was promptly stripped down and its powerful engine sold to a speedboat manufacturer who had developed the habit of never asking questions, at least not from hardfaced men willing to part with an expensive engine for a very fair price.

The theft was immediately reported to the police who, to Andrew's chagrin, immediately regarded him as the likeliest suspect.

'No, no, you can't be serious!' shouted the incredulous Andrew when it became clear to him that the bored sergeant behind the desk was convinced that the car was either not stolen at all, or that he was the brain behind the theft.

'Really, you must be joking. Some hoodlums grab my car at gunpoint in broad daylight and you now tell me that the car was not stolen after all. What kind of logic is that?'

'Who is saying anything about logic?' the policeman wanted to know. 'We are talking about a car which you alleged was stolen...'

'I did not allege anything' interrupted Andrew, his voice quivering with considerable emotion. ' My car was stolen by men wielding guns!'

'That is your story' insisted the policeman. 'Just give us time. We shall soon get to the bottom of this dirty business.'

The situation was clearly getting out of hand and it might have led to very unpalatable consequences. Most fortunately, Andrew's brother-in-law, a lawyer, who had been told of the theft of the car, arrived at the police-station, just as the poor man was making a statement preparatory to his being locked up on suspicion of arranging the spectacular theft of his own car.

After long and delicate negotiations, it was agreed that Andrew would make a certain hefty sum of money available "to facilitate police inquiries into the matter". For several weeks afterwards, Andrew was a very frequent caller at the police-station, but each time he was told that there was nothing to report. Of course there could be nothing to report since the dismembered parts of the car had long been disposed of. Whilst the police were going through the motions of looking for the car, its engine was hauling a large speed-boat through the huge rivers of the Niger delta. In other words, the car simply vanished without trace.

Andrew was still being milked over this incident when his daughter took ill. Some ruinously expensive medications were prescribed and administered to the poor girl who nevertheless resolutely refused to get better. Her exasperated father was on the verge of losing his mind when it was found that the drugs being administered were, to all intents and purposes, no more potent than chalk. Andrew had become one of the first victims of drug fakers in the country.

With life daily becoming more uncertain, the number of people living outside the law began to multiply at a truly alarming rate and there was no end to the tricks, which they hoped, would lift them out of the morass of common existence. The faking of drugs, of the pharmaceutical variety this time became quite common. The fakers could not afford the luxury of considering the consequences of their action and so the lives of most Nigerians were put at risk. It was only fortunate that the drugs with which the little girl was being treated were discovered to be fake. The poor man had to find money to buy a new set of drugs, this time taking care to make sure that these replacements were the genuine articles.

In the meantime, Mrs Andrew had fallen into the clutches of hire purchase merchants and a large chunk of her housekeeping allowance went towards paying for jewelry, clothes and fanciful shoes, which she could not afford and did not even need. This meant that not just Andrew, but every other member of his household had to make do with very little food of indifferent quality. The children had their growth stunted as a result and began to look reedy. Gone for good were those plump cheeks, which caused them to be noticed at the time that their parents brought them home from the USA.

At the same time, members of Andrew's extended family were making forceful demands, which could just not be ignored. The poor man's blood pressure began a dizzy climb into regions of poor health and still there were no signs of better times to come. To make matters worse, the Andrew family was ejected from their posh flat because he began to cheat on his employers by pocketing some of the money, which by rights belonged to them. In other words, he was living rather dangerously and his system was beginning to show unmistakable signs of strain. His greatest problem however was his landlord. The man was not interested in anything but money and he was not troubled by any scruples in connection with any activity, which made him richer. He had many houses and he was always building more, thereby increasing his not inconsiderable power over his less endowed fellow men. His rents had to be paid on time and he was not averse to charging all kinds of levies whenever he needed money for any purpose.

Not many of Andrew's co-tenants had any awareness of their rights under the law and so their landlord was able to get away with anything short of murder. It is from this point of view that one can appreciate the venom, which this man reserved for Andrew who not only knew his rights but also, insisted on being treated according to these rights. This did not do much for the poor man's blood pressure.

It was in the midst of all these troubles that Andrew's father-in-law, as inconsiderate as ever as far as Andrew was concerned, died. This was a calamity, not because the man died but because Andrew was expected to spend large sums of money in giving the man a befitting funeral. Poor Andrew was on the verge of falling into a pool of debt and there was no way of escaping a plunge into its murky depths now that he just had to come up with hefty sums of money within a very short time. Fortunately, borrowing money for a funeral was easier than anyone could have thought and so his blushes were spared by a loan, the size of which took Andrew's breath away.

The funeral itself turned out to be a very enjoyable function for the army of people whose only contribution to the festivities was their presence. There was plenty to eat and drink and the dancing was fast, furious and thoroughly enjoyable. It was at the height of the festivities that Andrew became aware of another pressing problem. One of the most visible guests was his landlord. Although there was little love lost between them, the landlord and his friends turned out in force to grace the occasion. And when the time came for the children of the deceased to take to the floor, Andrew's wife resplendent in expensive laces, which were not yet paid for was the focus of attention. The landlord and his friends showered the woman with so much money that she was in real danger of being buried under a deluge of high denomination currency notes. The poor woman, goaded beyond the bounds of reason threw all decorum to the winds and shook everything she had in the faces of her tormentors. For Andrew, the handwriting on the wall was clear and unmistakable. He had to run!

It was not very difficult for Andrew to convince his wife of the advisability of relocating to the USA where they were more likely to be found useful to the society and rewarded accordingly. Fortunately and thanks to the generosity of their besotted landlord, they found that not only were they able to pay off their numerous debts, they still had something left over with which to purchase one-way tickets out of the country. Andrew was on his way to prepare the way for the rest of the family when he ran into the officious gentleman from WAI. He appeared to have been dissuaded from checking out on that famous and often reported occasion. But it can now be revealed that Andrew's change of mind was very short-lived. He was back at the airport only a couple of days after the encounter with the man from WAI and this time he was successful in getting aboard a plane and checking out at last.

Andrew had a mission in the USA and that was to make money, a great deal of money so that when the time came, he could return to Nigeria with the wherewithal to set himself up in business and in doing so create opportunities for living the good life. This being so, he worked harder than most Americans did, which is saying a lot in a country with a high concentration of workaholics. Within a short time he had become a model citizen, with a powerful Mercedes-Benz and two other high profile cars in his garage. His children, including the little girl who had come so close to giving up the ghost in Nigeria were in the best and most expensive school that was available close to the leafy suburb where they lived. Even his wife, who was homesick more often than she thought she would be, was enjoying the good life. It looked as if they were set to continue to be the typical affluent family.

Life hardly moves along on a straight line and it did not do so in the case of Andrew. True he was getting everything he wanted but there came a time when everything, quite suddenly and inexplicably turned to dust and ashes in his mouth. He no longer enjoyed feeling the breeze on his face as he motored along on the freeways. He no longer noticed how well his apparently contented wife fed him and his children's brilliance in school did not appear to be as important as it once was. He began to sleep badly and it was not long before he started to lose weight noticeably. He was sure that there was nothing organically wrong with him but at the same time he knew that he really could not continue along the path he was currently treading.

It was not long before his condition became obvious and it was his wife who advised him to see a doctor.

'There is nothing wrong with me' was his airy initial response to this advice.

'True, there may be nothing wrong with you, but it is only reasonable for you to get that assurance from somebody who is qualified to give it.'

'Okay, I will see a doctor', he gave in with rather bad grace.

The family doctor was, like Andrew, a Nigerian in exile and any visit to him was more of a social occasion than a consultation. Whenever they got together, they talked about the terrible situation at home and the indignities, which they suffered at the hands of their reluctant hosts. It galled them that in spite of their evident success, they were still frequently treated like country bumpkins in town to lower the tone of the place.

After a thorough examination, the doctor duly confirmed that there was really nothing wrong with his patient. He was indeed able to assure Andrew that he was healthier than most people his age.

'Why do I feel the way I do then, if as you claim, there is nothing wrong with me?' he wanted very much to know.

'I have a strong feeling that all that is wrong with you is a rather bad attack of homesickness. If it is any consolation, I can tell you that you are the third Nigerian that I have seen with this condition this year.'

'I am not really homesick' he said after a long pause. 'I am not homesick in the sense that I want to go back home, but I am certainly not satisfied that being here is what is best for me. My children are not only growing up in a strange environment, they are daily growing away from me. They now regard themselves as being one hundred percent American, but I see that they have a mountain of disappointments ahead of them on this score. A friend of mine sleeps with a submachine gun under his bed, all because he has some very hostile neighbours, so it would appear as if being here is a mistake. On the other hand, the stories one hears about Nigeria are so bad, they are unbelievable. So, what is one to do under the circumstances?'

'I don't know. I really don't know' replied the doctor. 'It can be said that we are between a rock and a hard place. We cannot get any comfort whichever way we turn. But life has to go on so, my advice is that you protect yourself from stress as much as you can.'

Andrew went home as troubled as ever and talked the matter over with his wife. In the end it was decided that it was not enough that they sent dollars back home from time to time, Andrew had to go back home to monitor the situation on the ground there and find out if they could begin to make plans for a return.

As soon as this decision had been taken, Andrew was consumed by a fever of impatience to be off. Only a couple of weeks later, he was on the plane to Lagos. His first problem was that there were no more direct flights between the USA and Nigeria. There were no direct flights because the US government, ever concerned about the safety of her citizens had come to the inescapable conclusion that the airport in Lagos for a plethora of reasons, had become too dangerous for any of them to fly to. Andrew was irked by what he thought was a high-handed decision, but it was one that he could live with and so he took it in his stride.

Flying into Lagos just after dusk one balmy evening a little over ten years after "checking out" was an emotional experience. As soon as the plane taxied to a stop, Andrew was seized by a feeling of joy, the quality of which he had never experienced before. This was home, home at last and how good it was to be back. He quickly leapt to his feet, propelled by feverish impatience to set foot on home soil. He however just had to be patient as there were so many formalities that needed to be disposed of before he could get satisfaction.

The first thing that struck Andrew as he moved into the airport terminal was the wall of heat which enveloped him so that sweat spurted from his pores with impressive force. He was soon streaming with hot sweat. But this did not dampen his enthusiasm. Africa was a hot place and all those who could not stand the heat had no business being there. It suddenly sneaked into his mind however that the airport was fully air-conditioned the last time he passed through it on his way to exile. Obviously, the expensive central air-conditioner had broken down without anyone bothering to bring it back to life again.

All travellers have to go through Customs and Immigration at any international airport and Andrew was willing to submit himself to the ministrations of the relevant officials. What he went through in this his homeport was beyond anything he had experienced in any airport before. In the end, he was able to pass through Immigrations and Customs and was able to come out in the end because of the wad of greenbacks which he had the good sense to hand over to the aggressive officials that he had to deal with.

Lagos itself was a great shock to the returnee. Although he remembered how dirty the streets of Lagos were in the old days, he was shocked by what he saw around the city. Throughout the entire period of his visit, he could not take deep breaths for fear of being choked to death by noxious smells from gutters overflowing with every kind of filth. He just could not come to terms with the mountains of garbage, which blocked even the major roads. Moving around the city was a nightmare as the roads which were not blocked by refuse were mercilessly potholed, making progress extremely difficult even at the best of times.

Andrew spent two weeks in Lagos and in that time, he saw many things, which he just could not come to terms with. Only two days into his visit, he was caught in crossfire in a fire-fight between a determined gang of well-armed robbers and a combined police and army anti-crime patrol team in broad daylight. He cowered under his borrowed car as bullets buzzed around like a swarm of angry bees, furious at being disturbed in their major preoccupation of looking for nectar. Casualty reports were unreliable but an educated guess was that a total of nine men lost their lives in that skirmish which took place without the benefit of the cover of darkness. The black joke in Lagos was that armed robbers also loved to get a good night's sleep and so preferred to do their work in full glare of sunlight.

On another occasion, he was shocked almost out of his wits by television pictures of condemned robbers being done to death in batches by a firing squad doing their dirty work in the glare of public gaze. He felt physical pain and experienced deep psychological trauma as the mangled bodies of the executed men were carted away from the place of slaughter in a garbage disposal truck. There was no doubt that life was being lived in the raw. He listened with stark horror as a respected and responsible physician claimed on television that there were so many fake drugs on the market that it was not safe to assume that any of them could be relied on to effect any cures. He was afraid to ask after his young relatives after he was told that the police had killed one of them and another one had been driven insane by an acute lack of prospects. Yet another one was in police custody after she had been caught with heroin stuffed in a rather private portion of her anatomy. The only success story was of one of his nephews who was a football player with a team in the Belgian third division. The young footballer was home on holiday at the time of Andrew's visit and drove around town in a powerful BMW which he had bought cash down from one of the numerous roadside car dealers which dotted the city.

At the end of two weeks, Andrew feeling that his head was in serious danger of bursting went back to the USA through London.

For weeks after his return from Nigeria, Andrew walked around in a daze. It was as if his brain had been deprived of its ability to analyse the information fed into it. Besides, Andrew found it difficult to discuss his Nigerian trip with his wife. He just could not find the words to express his horror of the situation back where they used to call home. He was however quite clear in his mind that the sooner he stopped thinking of Nigeria as home, the sooner he would be able to get on with the rest of his life.

High Jinks in Rio

It was a very hot day but the heat could not penetrate the Senior Doctors' Room at the University Teaching Hospital. The room was kept cool by a new air-conditioner, which had been donated to the doctors by a local trader, described as 'filthy rich' by both his detractors and admirers. He had come into the hospital to have repairs to his anus which, being sorely troubled by the piles, made his life positively hellish. For all his money, life had turned into dust and ashes in his mouth. He was in deep despair and when the doctors, without any fuss restored equilibrium to his life by carving up his anal region and putting it together again, he registered his heart-felt gratitude by presenting the doctors with the superb air-conditioner. Now they too could get a little taste of the good life.

The room was both cool and uncharacteristically quiet on that warm afternoon. But, even if it was not quiet, Dr. Adebisi's whoop would have pierced the ears of everyone in the room. As it was, it startled everybody and all heads were turned in his direction. For a couple of minutes after disturbing the peace, in this manner, Dr. Adebisi remained the centre of attraction as his colleagues waited for him to intimate them with the reason or reasons for his obvious excitement.

'Great, great' was all they heard from their excited colleague who had got up, the better to savour whatever it was that had aroused him and what the message contained in the letter in his hand was about. They were sure it was not bad news anyway and that the message was from somewhere out of Nigeria because the envelope, which had fallen to the floor, was plastered over with some lurid and exotic stamps.

'Great, Brazil, here I come' shouted the good doctor and his friends knew immediately what had happened. For six weeks before then, they had heard nothing from their colleague that was not connected with Brazil. Dr. Tope Adebisi had applied for an invitation to attend a six-week seminar on Medical Statistics and he was very keen to go. Unfortunately, an invitation was simply not there for the taking as he had been warned that places on the seminar were very competitive, so competitive that only one place was reserved for all applicants from Nigeria. He knew that this place carried a high premium because he had been told that several dozen applications had been received from Nigerians who were every bit as qualified for the place as he was.

Attending the seminar was attractive in several ways. Apart from the opportunity to learn, it also meant part-sponsorship in foreign currency, something about as precious as flawless diamonds. And then, with all the problems attending everyday living in Nigeria, a six-week visit to Rio de Janeiro for any reason at all was something to look forward to.

Congratulations came in thick and fast and the good doctor beamed his acceptance.

'When are you going?' asked Biyi, his best friend.

'I must be there in another four weeks, or else my invitation will be revoked' replied Tope.

'You don't have much time then, so you had better get cracking so that you can get all your papers in order before then. Your passport is still okay, I take it.'

'Good Lord, no!' shouted Tope. 'I haven't been abroad for so long that I have allowed my passport to expire.'

'That means that you have only four weeks to get a new passport and then, a visa for Brazil. I am afraid, you have a job ahead of you' was Biyi's verdict.

Bisi, another doctor was called over. He, more than the others, was a man of the world and had the reputation for ferreting out all manner of information from the tightest bureaucratic corners. He was needed to give much needed advice as to how Tope would be able to put his travel papers in order within the short time available to him.

'The passport issue will be just as difficult as you want it to be.' he warned.

'Naturally, I want it to be as easy as possible' answered Tope.

Bisi gave a rueful smile before responding.

'In that case, you have to be prepared to pay much more for it than the official government rate and indeed, you have to avoid official lines all together. If you want to get your passport as early as tomorrow, it will be delivered to you here or even your house. On the payment of a hefty sum of money, of course.'

'What is your idea of a hefty sum?' asked Tola, the only lady there present.

'Well, depending on your connections, I will say that between ten and fifteen thousand Naira should do the trick.'

'Ten thousand Naira!' she shrieked, 'Why! That is what most of us earn in two months. Besides, everybody knows that the official rate is only five hundred Naira.'

'Yes' said Bisi wearily. 'Yes, I know that for five hundred Naira, you can have a brand new and authentic Nigerian passport, but let me assure you that should you choose to go through that route, you will still be waiting for your passport this time next year. First, there will be no forms available. When the issue of forms is somehow sorted out, in say three months, you will then be asked to go and bring a letter of identification from the chairman of your native Local Government Council. For you, I know that you will have to make a round trip of nearly nine hundred kilometres on mostly terrible roads. You will be very lucky to get the chairman to sign your form on your first visit, so you must be prepared to make two, or even three trips before you can come away with the precious signature. And that is not all! Your papers will then be sent to the police for their clearance and just how long that will take is anybody's guess. They have no computers and so they have to search laboriously through tons of files to make sure that you are not wanted anywhere in Nigeria for armed robbery, kidnapping, counterfeiting, or any such crimes. You will be lucky to have your papers from the police in anything under three months.'

'You must be joking!' one of his hearers burst out at this point.

'No, I am not joking' insisted Bisi. 'The situation is very bad, I assure you, because police clearance does not mean that your troubles are over. It will be highly unlikely that passport booklets will be available just when they are needed. The officials will tell you, with tears in their beady bureaucratic eyes that the supply of this commodity is fitful at best. They will say that they have to undertake frequent and perilous journeys to Abuja, many times at their own expense before they are successful in laying hands on about 25% of their requirements. Of course, they expect to be reimbursed by those wishing to be issued with passports. There are other minor points, which will each cause a delay of a couple of weeks here and there. Believe me, it is simply not worth the trouble to go through official channels.'

Tola was not amused by this grim picture. Indeed, she was indignant about it.

'It is people like you who give this country a bad name' she
hissed. 'I am a Nigerian just like you and I have never had to give
anyone a bribe. No, not one, and I daresay, I have not suffered any
ill-effects.'

'Who is talking about a bribe?' asked Bisi, his face shining with
mock astonishment. 'Did anyone hear me utter that dreadful word?
Let me say it loud and clear now, I have not asked anyone to bribe
anybody, neither in cash nor in kind.'

'What is the N10, 000 for then, if it is not a bribe?' retorted Tola
heatedly.

'Oh that!' responded Biyi dismissively. 'That is not a bribe. It is a
fee for services rendered. You doctors think you are the only people
who have the right to charge fees for services rendered. Well, you
are dead wrong. Many other people are performing useful services
for which they deserve to be paid. Winking a passport from the
Nigerian Immigration Service through whatever means is one such
service and believe me, it deserves a hefty payment.'

'And you tell me that you are not encouraging bribery and
corruption' responded Tola disgustedly.

'I don't have to sit here arguing with you. The choice is for Tope
to make. He may go to the officer in charge of protocol in the
university and collect a letter of introduction for the Chief Passport
Controller and start the process of getting a new passport through
official channels. Take it from me, the seminar will be long over by
the time that passport is issued. Alternatively, he may go and
negotiate an agreeable price with George in the Medical Records
Department and have his passport within 72 hours. The ball is in
Tope's court. Let him play it just as it pleases him. As for me, I am
going off to Ward C to see a very pretty young lady who is having a
torrid battle with typhoid. I will see you all later,' he concluded
breezily as he made for the door. But Tola was not going to allow
him to make an escape. No, not just yet.

'What of if Tope pays all that money and ends up with a fake
passport?'

Bisi laughed loud and brushed the suggestion aside.

'Ah, I don't expect honest people like you to understand that
there is honour among thieves. As long as Tope does not pay in
counterfeit bank notes, he will be given the real thing, a genuine
Nigerian passport on which he can travel confidently to any country
in the whole wide world. Now I really must go,' said Bisi as he

turned the door handle and this time left the room before Tola could think of any response.

There was however no doubt about which side won this verbal skirmish as very early the next morning, Tope was at the Registrar's office from where he collected a very nicely worded letter of introduction to the Chief Controller of Passports. The old man in charge of issuing such letters was on the verge of retiring after more than thirty years in the Registry. He believed in doing things in the old-fashioned way and so, Tope was received with grace and courtesy and his case treated with dispatch. This boosted his confidence in the intrinsic goodness of human nature. He would have gone away with a spring in his steps but for the fact that in bidding him farewell, the old man had wished him the very best of luck. Ordinarily, this should not have meant very much, if anything. But Tope could not help but notice that the wishes were expressed with so much feeling that he got the distinct impression that the old man was not just being polite. It was clear that he really needed a lot of luck if he was going to come away with his passport in the time available to him.

The next day, he was off to confront the dragons in the Passport Office with nothing more lethal in his armoury than the flimsy letter of introduction in his pocket and a fervent prayer on his lips. It had not been easy to get away from his duties at the hospital and under other circumstances, it would have been nearly impossible. But his colleagues were so keen to see him get away to Rio that he found a couple of them who were willing to cover for him.

The trip itself was quite uneventful and he got to the Passport Office long before it was due to open for business. This notwithstanding, he found that at least, a score of people had got there before him. A substantial number of these very early arrivals showed signs of having slept on the premises. These were the people who had come a very long way and had arrived in town the night before having learnt from bitter experience that only the earliest birds stood the chance of catching any worms in the Passport Office.

Tope waited with the other applicants and listened with a sinking heart and rising alarm as the others, most of whom could be regarded as old-timers swapped stories and compared notes in respect of their various experiences at the hands of the officials of the Passport Office. Many of these had in fact met on the premises so often that they had gone past the state of being fellow-sufferers or casual acquaintances and had become friends.

Although Tope's faith in the eventual successful outcome of his mission was dented by these stories, it was not shaken, especially since none of the others had come there on the strength of an introduction of 'an influential person', the registrar of a university, as he had done. He could not help but notice that most of the others were barely literate and he really could not find it possible to censure the officials who were making it difficult for persons such as they to get a passport. Now, he was different, very different. Or, at least he thought he was. He was not just educated but very much so. He was also a practising doctor in one of the nation's most prestigious institutions and as the letter in his pocket had stated, he was going to attend an important seminar, 'from which not only Dr. Adebisi, but the entire Nigerian healthcare delivery system is bound to derive immense benefits'. Surely, the officials were bound to be very helpful, if not for his own personal interest, for the sake of the much-battered Nigerian healthcare delivery system.

The hopeful applicants were kept waiting for another half-hour after the official opening time before they were allowed to enter the hallowed precincts of the Passport Office. By this time, they were in excess of one hundred men, women and children who immediately swarmed into the building and spread through it like a column of soldier ants that had been disturbed on the march. Many of them had come armed with letters from particular officers and they homed in on their prospective saviours hoping to get things done through such contacts. Others had become such regular visitors that they had made friends with some of the more strategically placed officers. And there were yet others who were professional passport facilitators, or in plain language, touts who had made a living from their ability to help applicants cut through the red tape artfully tied to frustrate their aspiration in the direction of becoming proud owners of a Nigerian passport.

Tope had a letter for the top man and he saw no reason to dilly-dally with mere lackeys. He went straight up to the office of the Chief Controller and confidently expected to be given speedy satisfaction.

The first shock for him was that by the time he found his way to the office, there were eight other hopefuls waiting. He had no idea how they had got there so fast, but there could be no doubting the evidence of his eyes even if they were round with surprise. In any case, he did not think he needed to join the queue since he was there on the authority of one who was greater than most. He therefore went up to the boss' secretary and said a hearty good-morning.

Her response to his greeting was barely audible, but her question was not.

'What can I do for you?' she asked, her voice carefully devoid of any eagerness to be of help.

'I have a letter here from the Registrar of my university for the Controller' replied Tope, his tone of voice just short of being unpardonably imperious, so confident was he of making a telling impression.

The lady was resolutely unimpressed. She had dealt with many people who had brought letters from all manner of powerful men and women and she had come to regard letters from university registrars as not being dealt from the top of the deck.

'Hmmm, I see', she mumbled. 'Well, the Controller is yet to come in for the day, so you are advised to wait for him on the queue outside, or you leave the letter with me and I will take it in to him when he comes.'

'You don't seem to understand...' Tope was about to launch into some detailed explanation, when the lady cut in very smartly.

'I understand all right, you know. No doubt you are a university lecturer who needs a passport and you have a letter of recommendation from your university. We get dozens of such letters every month and I am only trying to be helpful by advising you to wait to see the Controller yourself. Ordinarily, I will simply take the letter from you and send it on to the Controller with all the other letters this afternoon, so please don't disturb my peace this morning. Just do what you are told.'

A very warm retort rose to Tope's tongue, but he had the presence of mind to suppress it and even wish the lady a good-morning. He left her office and took his place on the queue as he had been advised to do. In the meantime the queue had grown considerably longer in his absence.

The people in front of the Controller's office had to wait for the better part of one hour before the owner of the office finally put up an appearance. A volley of greetings from his subordinates marked the big man's arrival. They were all eager to ingratiate themselves with the man in charge. Their greetings were acknowledged by a wave here, a smile there and the very occasional verbal response.

The supplicants around the Controller's office quickly made way for him to get to his door. A strikingly light-skinned lady, flaunting a blatantly sexy bottom encased in a pair of stonewashed designer jeans, into which she appeared to have been poured and allowed to set, accompanied him. No full-blooded male could have remained unmoved in the face of such provocation. The pair was wafted into the office by waves of expensive perfume and the door closed after them. Thereafter, the door remained closed for another half-hour during which only infrequent peals of feminine laughter betrayed the occupancy of the office. Eventually, tired of whatever game that was being played, the Controller flung open his door and began to attend to business.

Another frustrating hour crawled by before Tope was finally allowed to see the Controller and his female companion who sat reading a magazine in one corner of the room. Pressing firmly on the lid of the anger threatening to boil out of him, Tope wished the Controller a good-morning and to his surprise, he got a warm response.

'Well, what can I do for you', beamed the Controller.

'I am Dr. Adebisi and I have a letter for you from Mr. Adetunji'

'Who is Mr. Adetunji?'

'The Registrar of...'

'Oh, that Mr. Adetunji', cut in the Controller. 'You really did not need to see me. We have an officer downstairs who deals with letters from institutions such as yours. I will just minute on the letter, now that I have seen it and I think it will be best if you took the letter down to Mrs. Karimu yourself. It is not safe to trust any of our messengers with it' he concluded with a surprisingly self-satisfied chuckle.

'Is that all?' asked the bewildered Tope as he was dismissed.

'Oh yes', replied the Controller. 'Mrs. Karimu will take very good care of you.'

The prophecy was soon found to be hollow.

Mrs. Karimu turned out to be a fat, bitter lady on the wrong side of middle-age who at first sight appeared to be some lucky person's favourite aunty. She was nothing of the sort. After many years in the civil service, she was still without any real responsibility and she resented this with a vengeance. Most of her venom was reserved for promising young men and more pointedly, women who appeared bound for the top.

'Yes, what can I do for you?' Mrs. Karimu barked with real menace as Tope was led into the cubicle, which served as her office, by a suitably reverent messenger.

'Good-morning, Ma'am' responded Tope, hoping desperately that her bark was worse than her bite.

'I have a letter here for the Controller, but he has sent me on to you' he said as he proffered that important document.

Mrs Karimu took the letter and scanned it.

'Hmm, I see', she spat. 'You lecturers are always flitting about instead of staying at home and doing the job for which you are being paid. Now what is it that you are looking for in Brazil, of all places?' Just as if she knew anything about Brazil.

'I have been invited to a seminar there', he responded calmly, just as if he cared anything for her opinion.

'Seminar!' she snorted, packing as much scorn into that single word as most people will just manage to fit into two long sentences.

'Seminar indeed! I bet you are going there to have a high good time at government expense, and what more, you are bound to be paid very handsomely for that privilege. I see that you have been in the university for quite some time so what benefit are you going to derive from this junket? In any case, there is nothing I can do for you until you have filled the prescribed form and I am afraid, there are no forms available right now' she concluded on a ringingly triumphant note.

'I really cannot believe that you don't have any forms in this office', his voice rising in spite of his earlier determination to keep his temper in check.

'Frankly, I don't care what you believe', her voice shrill with impatience. 'All I know is that there are no forms here, and that is that. Besides, we are unlikely to have any forms for a long time to come, so you can do whatever you please.'

'But I saw some people with forms only a few minutes ago' replied Tope in a tone of voice stiff with irritation.

'Look', Mrs Karimu shot back with great heat, 'it is not my business to sit here and waste time arguing about the availability or otherwise of some miserable forms. If you saw anybody with the forms you need, then they are the ones you need to talk to. Those are the people who can tell you how to get your own form. Find a form, fill it and then come back here, maybe I will be able to do something for you then', she concluded with a negligent wave of a plump hand.

These words slammed into Tope with the force of heavy stones flung at him by very strong arms. The furious glances with which he hoped to score some points off his formidable opponent were a dead loss. As soon as the last word dropped off her rubbery lips and bounced round the room, she turned all her attention to a comic magazine with which she had been amusing herself before the importunate visitor intruded into her air space.

Tope, on the verge of giving in to the homicidal thoughts crowding into his mind, walked out of Mrs Karimu's office to go and act on her advice and find someone who could tell him how to acquire a passport form in what was touted to be the Passport Office.

He did not have to go far to find somebody. No sooner did he shake the hostile dust of his tormentor's office off his shoes did he run into one of the people with whom he had been waiting for the office to open. Clutched in his sweaty right hand was a passport form.

'Eh, my friend, how is it that you have been able to get yourself one of these forms? I have just been told that there are none available within this building.'

'Your informant was quite correct. There are no forms in this building' was his new friend's terse response.

'Then how come you have one in your possession?' asked Tope rather aggressively.

'Be patient and I will tell you' he was advised. 'If you turn right at the road junction just up the street from here, you will find a green one-storey building. Go up to the first floor and ask for Alhaji. He will give you a form.'

'Just like that?' asked Tope.

'Of course not!' snapped the man. 'You will have to part with the sum of N750 for the rare privilege of handling a Nigerian passport form.'

'This is incredible' countered Tope. 'It says on that board in black and white that you don't have to pay anything to obtain a form. You should only bring N500 when you come back to submit the filled form.'

'Do you think I can't read?' asked the man crossly. 'I know that you don't have to pay anything for the form, but this is my third visit here and I was no nearer to getting a form than I was on my first one. I would even now have been chasing shadows had some Good Samaritan not shown me the way. You may quibble over N750 but believe me, that is no more than half of what I have spent so far in transport and other fares since I began my quest for a passport almost four weeks ago. I wish somebody had directed me to the Alhaji on my first visit here and spared me all the trouble that I have gone through over the matter of this form -- are you going to see the Alhaji, or not?'

'I am afraid I can't go and see the Alhaji even if I wanted to. I had not thought that I had to pay anything' replied Tope who at this stage was feeling well and truly whipped by these unexpected turns of events.

Tope went up to the Doctors' Room as soon as he got back. Coincidentally, all those who were present when the fateful letter from Brazil was received were also there to hear the report of Tope's experiences. All the hearers except one were moved to pity by the poor fellow's tales of woe. No prizes for guessing that the exception was Bisi, who far from feeling any sympathy, had to struggle very hard not to give in to the sort of laughter which was fairly choking him.

Bisi struggled hard to no avail. As Tope came to the end of his story, Bisi gave in and burst into loud laughter.

'I was quite sure that Tope was wasting his time when I was told that he had gone off to the Passport Office. You people are still living in the past, a past that has gone up in smoke. Let me assure you that the past, that time long ago when there was a measure of sanity in the affairs of this country is dead. Take it from me, this place is now a trackless jungle and unless you learn the ropes, you will soon be devoured by a big, bad wolf. No wonder your precious Mrs.Karimu wanted to bite you. She probably eats two or three innocents like you for breakfast. Get wise my friend and go and negotiate with George. Your only hope of getting to Brazil is George!'

Nobody said anything, or more correctly, nobody could say a word for a charged couple of minutes. Even Tola who had been so truculent in her defence of the proper way of doing things remained resolutely silent.

It was Tope, the man in the middle of it all who broke the unnatural silence.

'I cannot afford to part with N10, 000' he wailed.

'Do you mean that you do not have that amount of money, or that you cannot afford to spend it on a passport?' asked Bisi.

'What is the difference between the two?' asked Tola who had suddenly found her voice

'There is a great deal of difference' Bisi replied. 'If he does not have the money, then there is nothing he can do and that is that. However, he may have N10, 000 but may not be able to spend it because it is already committed to some other project. My advice is that if he has the money, he should spend it on a passport and consider it a safe investment. He only needs to get approval to buy foreign exchange at the official rate and then come back from Brazil and sell it for nearly four times what he paid for it on the black market. That is what all who have access to foreign exchange are doing and Tope had better get on the bandwagon. It may be his only chance. In any case, I was so sure that Tope was going to run into a brick wall over this passport issue that I have already approached George on his behalf. He told me that if Tope was willing to wait for one week, he would be able to swing the deal for N8, 500.

'But you said that George needed only 72 hours to come up with a passport the other day' Tola reminded him and all the others.

'If Tope can come up with N15, 000, the time lapse will remain at 72 hours. Under normal circumstances, he would have had to wait for longer than one week but, according to George, Tope was helpful to his sister, or was it his aunty, and since then he had been looking for a way of showing his gratitude. This is certainly one of those times when it pays to be a doctor.'

Tope had nothing to say, but he had come to accept that there was no way he could get a passport without George's help. So to George he went for prompt satisfaction.

Tope was very pleased that the passport problem had been solved. However, the issue of sponsorship was still to be tackled. He now knew that a pot of gold waited for him in Brazil, but the pot was of no use to him unless he could somehow find his way over there to claim it. As Bisi had so correctly put it, he had to regard the Brazil trip as an investment. The least expensive item of expenditure was the passport. There were several other items which, to use the language of business, were more capital intensive. He needed an airline ticket without which he could not get a visa from the Brazilian embassy and he needed at least $1,000 to convince the Brazilians that he was a man of substance and was not likely to disappear into the jungles of Rio once the seminar was over. He had no intention of spending any of this money in Brazil as he was resolved to live very frugally indeed throughout the period of the seminar. He planned to come back home with a load of genuine American dollars, which would represent very generous returns on his investment. At least that was the outline of his plans on paper. He still had to find a sponsor to start the ball rolling.

Tope's Brazil adventure quickly became something of a preoccupation with his colleagues who were very free and generous with their advice as to how to find a suitable sponsor. Capable sponsors were however very thin on the ground and landing one was clearly going to be a very tough proposition.

One obvious sponsor was the university, which was supposed to have set aside some money for the use of lecturers wishing to attend conferences and other such academic events anywhere in the world. This money was administered by a supposedly high-powered Senate committee with the Chairman, Committee of Deans as its chairman. Despite the impressive calibre of the members of this committee, it was chronically and drastically short of funds. Nevertheless, Tope collected the relevant application forms, filled them in triplicate and submitted these to the secretary to the committee. Being well-aware of the parlous state of the committee's finances, the secretary advised Tope to have a chat with the chairman of the committee, especially since there was such little time within which his application had to be processed.

Tope was graciously received by the chairman, maybe because there was very little to offer thereafter.

'This is a very good case,' admitted the chairman. 'It is most unfortunate that there is nothing we can do to help you. You see, we have a very serious problem here. We were given N2 million to disburse to applicants, but at today's prices, that sum of money can only purchase about twenty tickets to London. We had no less than two hundred and sixteen applications for overseas conferences last year and we are expected to give money to cover both travelling and living expenses so you can appreciate the enormity of our problem. Somebody applied to us for sponsorship to a conference in

Tokyo and if we had approved his request, we would have spent more than half of that money to satisfy him. As things stand, we have decided that it has become unreasonable to sponsor overseas trips until further notice and even then, we still have to turn down more than 70% of applicants for local conferences.'

At this point Tope wanted to know what was being done to bring about some improvement in the situation.

'The truth is that, there is very little that can be done. We have tried to get the Development Committee to vote more funds for the Learned Conferences Committee, but all the members are also members of the Development Committee and are only too well-aware of the fact that the university is knee-deep in debt. There is simply no money available within the university.'

'But, what can I do?' burst out Tope in desperation. 'This seminar is very important to me and by attending, I will also become more useful to my colleagues who need to analyse the data from their various research projects. Most of the cost of this seminar will be borne by my hosts and the least the university can do is to pay my air fare.'

'There can be no denying the strength of your case. It is just that the university is not in any position to give you any satisfaction in this matter', responded the professor wearily. He then went on after wiping purely imaginary sweat from his brow. 'I really hate having to do this job. Everyday, and sometimes, several times a day, I have the unpleasant duty of trying to explain to people why their application for funds has to be turned down. Not because they lack merit, but because we are operating a system which has a great, big hole where its heart should be.'

It was clear that the poor man was in real pain, so much so that Tope felt a twinge of sympathy for the poor man who had not learnt how to say no to requests which were obviously beyond h᠎is powers to address. Nevertheless, Tope could not give up. At least, not at that point.

'You may not be able to help me in your official capacity, but can't you do something for me unofficially? What I mean is, do you know anybody outside the university system that can be of use to me?'

'Well,' responded the professor, brightening up at the prospect of being useful at last. 'Have you thought of approaching the Director of Medical Statistics in the Federal Ministry of Health?'

'No, I haven't. I had no idea that I could get anything from that quarter' answered Tope.

'I am sure that one or two of your colleagues have received funds for the purpose of attending conferences abroad from a department in the Ministry of Health in the past so I think you should explore the possibility of getting what you want from there. What I can do is to give you a note to one of my friends that is a director in that ministry and he will be able to advise you appropriately.'

'Excuse me sir, but do you think that your friend will be willing to help me?' Tope had suffered too much in the hands of members of the great Nigerian civil service not to be wary of an encounter with anybody even remotely connected with that organisation.

'Ah, you have nothing to fear on that score', assured the professor. 'I am sending you to Kola. He was my classmate in the secondary school and I have no doubt that he will do all he can for you.'

Tope was in desperate need of cheer and this appeared to be just what he needed.

'Thank you very much' he gushed. 'You have rekindled the hope which I was sure was dead only a few minutes ago. How soon can I get the letter?'

'You can get it immediately. I don't have to write an official letter to Kola. I will scribble a note to him and that should be enough. Just make yourself comfortable whilst I write the note.'

As far as Tope was concerned, this was great news indeed and as the professor wrote, or as he put it, scribbled his little note which in the end, ran to three pages, he began to dream of Brazil and the opportunities which awaited him there. As a student, he had paid very little attention to Statistics, but as a researcher he had come to appreciate the power of this analytical tool. His interest was further developed when he found that most of his colleagues thought that all there was to Statistics was calculating averages. As the expert statistician among them, the call on his services was very heavy. What the others did not know was that there was still a great deal about the subject that was Greek to him. And he was hopeful that at the end of his exposure in Brazil, he would be much more confident about his ability to juggle all those masses of figures.

'The very best of luck to you', said the Prof. as he handed over the letter. I am always pleased to see that in spite of the serious problems we have to grapple with, some of you, the younger academics are still in there struggling to put things together. You are the only hope for this system, so don't give up.'

'Thank you very much. I will always be grateful to you for this' Tope assured the older man before walking out of the office with a spring in his step. He actually just managed to restrain himself from breaking into a jig. So pleased was he by what he took to be great success.

Two days later, Tope was on his way to Lagos armed with a plethora of advice.

'You cannot go to any of those ministries in Lagos casually dressed,' warned Eddy, one of Tope's self-appointed mentors. 'Listen to me now', Eddy went on, 'Lagos is a place where appearance counts for everything. You have to go there in your best suit and make sure that your shirt, tie and socks are colour coordinated. That way, when those snobbish Lagos gatemen see you, they will know straightaway that they are in the presence of a man of substance. Otherwise, you may not be allowed to even take a step across their threshold.'

'You seem to have forgotten that I have a letter for a Director in the Ministry' Tope pointed out.

'This is precisely why I am worried about you' moaned Eddy. 'You are too trusting, far too trusting for your own good. What do you think is the business of those people with letters when they can't even read? Who is to know about your letter if it is simply confiscated by the porter? He will straightaway throw your letter in the dustbin, or chew it up into pulp and swallow it, swearing thereafter that he had never in his life set eyes on you or your precious letter. Be warned. That letter is for Mr Kola Dabo. Make sure you put it into his hand and nobody else's. Don't even give it to his secretary. There is no guarantee that she will pass it on to him.'

'What if Mr Dabo is not in the office when I call?' asked Tope.

'You will just have to go back there again' responded Eddy very firmly.

'This business is likely to take too much of my time' grumbled Tope.

'You won't think so once you get to Brazil, so don't moan about that,' said Eddy.

'What you should keep very clear in your mind is that Mr Dabo is your real passport to Brazil and you must guard that letter with everything you've got. You must not lose it.'

'Lose it!' shouted Tope. 'Forget it, there is no way this letter can get out of my hand unless it is to put it in Mr Dabo's hands.'

On the appointed day, Tope was at the Ministry of Health early enough to have arrived before some of the tardier members of the staff of the ministry showed up for work. He found out soon enough however that he need not have bothered since a large notice announced to all the world that no visitors were allowed on the premises before 10.00 am. He therefore had to loiter outside the building for quite some time before the gates were flung open to allow the ingress of a strong wave of human beings who were determined to transact all manner of businesses, not all of them legal, within the ministry on that particular day. Most of them were very elegantly dressed and Tope was grateful to Eddy for his advice concerning the manner of his dressing.

Tope found out that Mr Dabo's office was all the way up on the twelfth floor and a porter who secured the services of a young clerk in Mr Dabo's office to act as a guide to the visitor made getting there easy for him. They made the trip in a lift whose condition suggested that it was much older than the building in which it was being operated. Tope was indeed convinced by all the banging and rattling which accompanied their ascent that the lift had been bought second hand at a lift jumble sale. Even at the best of times, he was very wary of taking a lift in a country where power cuts were inexplicably frequent and where there was the dangerous and widespread belief that maintenance of machines and buildings was a waste of time and money. The prevailing philosophy was "if it ain't broke, don' fix it" and so Tope was accompanied on the lift by fears that the lift was going to get stuck somewhere between the seventh and eighth floors and suffer the agony of being trapped in there for most of the day. The careless manner with which his guide lounged in one corner of the creaking lift did not reassure the poor man that all would be well. And so it was with great relief that he got off when the ancient contraption stopped and its doors creaked open to disgorge its human cargo on the twelfth floor.

As to be expected of the office of such an important man, Mr Dabo's office was fairly crowded out with people who could only be supplicants for one favour or the other. Most of them, like Tope, were clutching letters of introduction from people who could claim some form of acquaintance however faint or distant with Mr Dabo. They had come with hopes in their hearts to get jobs for which they were not remotely qualified or land contracts, which they had no competence to prosecute. They were all to be attended to and Tope had resigned himself to a very long wait on seeing that crowd. In any case, he had to register his presence with the secretary.

'Good-morning, madam' Tope, well-aware of the authority of secretaries said to the fiercely painted lady in question. She looked like an accomplished practitioner of the art of shrivelling presumptuous supplicants with nothing more lethal than a glance and Tope had to get a firm grip on himself in order not to be intimidated by the person under the many layers of war paint on her face. Appearances often give the lie to the character as Mr Dabo's secretary turned out to be very friendly. He was of course asked to fill the mandatory visitor's form and as soon as she noticed Tope's title, she wanted to know if he had a doctorate degree to his name or that he was "a doctor who treated people in hospital."

'I am really both,' replied Tope, warming up to his interrogator. 'I am a doctor of medicine who has a Ph.D.'

'I see' replied the lady who was impressed no end by this piece of information. 'I am sure that my boss will be happy to see you. Doctors are his favourite people especially now that his daughter is also one. I will tell him that you wish to see him and I am pretty sure that he will attend to you straightaway.'

'Thank you very much' replied Tope. 'I was thinking that I would have to wait a long time and I have come from rather far away to see him. I have a letter here from Professor Longe who was his classmate. It is about sponsorship for a trip abroad.'

'Don't worry about a thing. I know that he will make time to see you very soon' she predicted confidently.

Her prediction was spot on as she soon emerged from the office and asked Tope to go in to see her boss who was clearly pleased to see his visitor.

They exchanged very warm greetings and the all-important letter was reverently handed over to the addressee who straightaway slit it open and read the contents very carefully. This exercise took the best part of ten minutes. Finally, Mr Dabo looked up with a warm smile.

'So, you are well-acquainted with my old friend, Sola.'

For a second, Tope wondered who Sola was, but fortunately, his brain quickly flashed the message that Sola must be the Chairman, Committee of Deans, the man on whose ticket he was travelling.

'Yes sir', was his eager response

'We have known each other for years and I am always very happy to hear from him. About your application for sponsorship, my advice is that you approach the Public Health Department. They have a lot of money under their direct control and should be able to make a couple of thousand dollars available to you. Forget about the Statistics people. They are so preoccupied with their figures that they are not too good at fighting for the funds, which are available for distribution among the various departments. Besides, the Public Health Department receives grants from many foreign donors and they can always list you as one of their experts. You need to settle this issue very quickly, so let me send you along to Dr Cole, the head of that department. Let me know how you get on with him, but I am fairly certain that you will be well-looked after.'

An electric bell was used to summon a messenger, a garrulous young man who, in the five minutes that it took to bring Tope to Dr Cole's office had told the doctor about all the aches and pains, which afflicted his grandmother, in the confident expectation of a prescription. He was not upset when he was informed that such second party consultation was unworkable and volunteered to wait until the doctor had finished his business so that he could give a fuller description of his grandmother's numerous ailments. It was not easy to dissuade him.

Dr Cole's office, unlike Mr Dabo's was not under siege from visitors and Tope was indeed given the impression that he was most welcome. The secretary, looking distinctly bored was happy to see another human face and she flashed him a dazzling smile.

Unfortunately, Dr Cole was not in the office but according to the secretary, he was expected back within the hour and he was invited to make himself comfortable as he waited for his host to arrive. Tope was most favourably impressed by his reception. So far, nobody he had met had conformed to the stereotype of the obnoxious public official whom his colleagues with good intentions it must be said had warned him to expect. He was served with tasty biscuits and tea as he waited for Dr Cole's imminent arrival. He had been waiting for just over half an hour and was into the second article in the fifteen-month old copy of the Lancet which he found on the low table in front of him when a tall, disarmingly handsome man dressed in a very well-cut suit sauntered into the room.

'Welcome back, Doctor. This gentleman, Dr Adebisi, has been waiting to see you' announced the secretary as soon as she saw the new-comer.

This was without doubt the much sought after Dr Cole. At the very first sight, he did not make a favourable impression on Tope who had always felt that medicine was a very serious business. As far as he was concerned, there was no place in the profession for obvious dandies like Dr Cole. That day he was wearing a grey suit, which appeared to have cost much more than a civil servant could afford. The heavy and expensive ring on Dr. Cole's right index finger and the very flat gold watch, which adorned his left wrist, did nothing to calm Tope's disquiet.

'Good-morning Doctor' drawled Dr Cole as he consulted his expensive watch as if to confirm that it was not yet noon.

'Good-morning, Sir' replied Tope with exaggerated politeness. In his experience, such people needed to be handled gingerly and he was not about to allow the problem of an overblown ego spoil his chances.

'Come into my office where we can be comfortable' invited Dr Cole as he held the door open so that Tope could go in.

On entering the room, Tope could see immediately that it was furnished more to provide comfort than to make serious work possible within it. Indeed it looked more like the lounge of an exclusive club than an office. There was a suite of plush furniture and beautiful paintings on the walls. The temperature in the room was maintained at a comfortable value by a powerful air-conditioner, which purred like a well-fed and thoroughly domesticated cat. The only item of furniture, which suggested that the room served as an office, was a massive desk in the far corner. It did not look as if much work was done on it. Clearly, the occupant of that office liked comfort to the point of indulgence.

'Now, what can I do for you?' asked Dr Cole as the two men settled into their respective chairs.

'I need sponsorship', was the prompt response.

'For what?' came the logical question to this bald statement.

'To attend a seminar on Medical Statistics in Brazil.'

'I see. But why have you come to me? This is not a sponsoring agency.'

'I know that and would not have come to see you but I was advised to do so by Mr. Dabo. I think I should explain fully' said Tope.

'Please do' invited Dr Cole.

Tope had told his story so many times that by this time he had become word perfect and needed just a little less than five minutes to put Dr Cole in the picture.

'Do you mean that things are now so bad in our universities that lecturers can no longer attend conferences?' asked Dr Cole in considerable alarm.

'Lecturers cannot do anything but teach these days and even then, they do not have the materials to do even this properly. We are only struggling to keep the university system alive somehow, in the hope that it can be revived in the future.'

'What is this country coming to?' fumed Dr Cole.

'I don't know' replied Tope, thinking that the question demanded an answer.

'Right now, I am preoccupied with finding a solution to my immediate problem. I know that there is plenty of time within which to worry about where the country is going to, or even if it is going anywhere.'

'I see what you mean and normally I would have been able to help you. I am willing to help, but it would be very difficult for me to do anything for you right now. You see, my department is rather short of ready cash at the moment.'

'But sir, I was made to understand that your department is very well-funded from both local and international sources' said Tope, despair clearly written on his face.

'Under normal circumstances, your needs would have been taken care of, but present circumstances are about as far from normal as they are ever likely to get. You see, we have, in the last six months been battling with major outbreaks of cerebrospinal meningitis in the north and cholera just about throughout the length and breadth of the country and trying to cope with these have drained our resources. International donors are not as eager as they used to be about giving us assistance, at least in cash as they used to do. For some reason, they have taken to giving us vehicles, which are difficult to maintain adequately. Many of them are in the yard behind us just gathering rust. As for the subvention from the government, the less said, the better. According to the budget, we have more than N20 million coming to us, but only goodness knows when we will see the money' Dr Cole concluded bitterly.

The two men were silent for a couple of minutes, each of them apparently lost in gloomy thought.

'Is there anything, anything at all that can be done for me?' Tope finally broke the now uncomfortable silence.

'Well, I am basically an optimist' beamed Dr Cole, suddenly cheerful again.

'Never say die is my motto and believe me, I think your case is good, so good that I will support it as much as I am able to. Our pecuniary difficulties are actually only temporary and there is nothing to suggest that they will not be removed very soon.'

'But I don't have time! I must be in Brazil in three weeks, or lose my place!' cried Tope.

'Three weeks!' echoed Dr Cole. 'I see what you mean. Still, three weeks is a long time and there is no saying what will happen as early as next week. But then, nothing positive may happen for another six weeks. The thing to do is to keep trying and not give up.'

'You said something might happen soon. What do you mean by that?'

Dr Cole gave a tight little smile, trying to give the impression that being an outsider, Tope was not likely to understand what exactly was going on. Finally, he nodded as if he had come to a decision.

'The ways of the civil service are truly mysterious and there are so many wheels turning other wheels that it is sometimes very difficult to know which wheel is turning and which one is being turned. I doubt that you can properly appreciate what we doctors in administrative positions here are going through. Apart from personal and interdepartmental rivalries, there are many forces, some of them very remote with which we are forever in conflict. The point you have to be clear about is that the battle for available resources is continuous and fierce. They are also frequently bloody. You see, available resources are not enough to go round. Take the case of our annual subvention. Our budget is N63 million, but only N21 million was approved. Now, this is still a healthy sum and if I had that money under my control, I would be glad to sponsor your trip. Unfortunately, I don't have it because some officials in the Treasury have impounded it, so to speak.'

'Why would they want to do that?' asked Tope.

'Oh, they have their reasons, but that is of no importance. All I want is that this money be released so that my department may be able to get on with its work.'

'For how long are they likely to hang on to this money?'

'For as long as it pleases, but I think that the money will be made available just as soon as I pay them, or rather, bribe them with ten percent of the sum due to the department.'

Tope gasped. He just could not believe what he had just been told in such a casual manner by a very senior official of the federal government of Nigeria.

'How can that be?' he managed to croak.

Dr Cole, wiser by far in the wicked ways of the world just smiled and waved his manicured hands in an expansive gesture.

'That is the way it is these days, and there is nothing that can be done about it.'

'Is this sort of thing not against the law?'

'The law? What is that? It just does not exist for powerful people and you can hardly get more powerful than those fat cats in the Treasury. I am afraid that there is no way I can get my departmental allocation without paying them their cut upfront as they say these days. In the days when we got substantial grants from foreign sources, there was no difficulty about meeting demands like this, but times have changed even if the Treasury refuses to acknowledge this sad fact of life.'

'The country is finished,' said Tope sadly, shaking his head in real despair.

'I won't be so sad if I were you' advised Dr Cole. 'This sort of thing goes on all over the world. If you do go to Brazil and you know where to look there, you will find a great deal of corruption, and in the most unlikely places too.'

'That is no consolation. From what I have seen and heard in the last few days, the mechanism of administration in this country is shot through with corruption. In other countries, corrupt people have to carry on their activities underground. Here, it is the other way round. Those who are working honestly are in real danger of being swept aside, or even into prison, there to learn the error of their ways at their leisure.'

'You are right,' agreed Dr Cole, 'but I still say you should not give up hope. Good things can still happen in this country and as for your trip, anything can happen in the next few days. Why don't you let me have all your papers so that I can set about trying to get you what you want.'

'Are you saying that there is some hope that I will get sponsorship?' asked Tope, his voice strengthened by hope.

'Oh yes. The situation is not hopeless. You can take it that the answer at this point is maybe, which is a sight better than no.'

'Thank you very much,' said Tope with feeling as he handed over his papers.

Dr. Cole leafed through the sheaf of papers, examining each one as if to satisfy himself that they were all genuine.

'Yes' he said at last. 'All the necessary papers are here. The only thing that you have to do now is to write a formal letter of application for sponsorship to me, or more correctly, the Head, Department of Public Health. You may have reasons not to think very much of civil service procedures, especially judging by what we have been talking about, but believe me all our work here will be grounded if we cannot produce all supporting documents for the smallest item of expenditure when the auditors come calling.'

Under other circumstances, Tope would have been amused about quibbling over a couple of hundred thousand Naira when over N2 million can be used for an unitemised, and indeed unitemisable purpose. At that time, he was far too disgusted to be amused and just got on with writing the application. He could not leave the subject alone however and just had to ask how the bribe would be described in the books.

'Oh, there is no problem about that,' said Dr Cole in a decidedly offhand manner. 'We will simply put it down as an item of public relations.'

'Public relations!' shouted Tope in disbelief.

'Yes. Public relations' confirmed Dr Cole, convincing Tope of the futility of further questions on that subject.

'When should I come back to check up on the progress of my application?' he asked, by way of changing the subject of their conversation.

Dr Cole made a great show of thinking about what to say before suggesting that Tope should come back the following week, even though there was no guarantee that he would have a definite answer for him at that time. Tope told him that he understood and that since he really had no choice, he just had to keep his fingers crossed.

Back home, the other doctors were quite sure that Dr Cole would come up with the goods. All of them, except Eddy that is. He was resolutely skeptical about the eventual successful outcome of the situation.

'You are too trusting, Tope' he shouted in exasperation, 'you are too trusting and you are sure to be disappointed. I feel it. I know it. That man is going to do you down somehow. Don't ask me how he is going to do it, but prepare yourself for a big let-down. It is totally out of character for a Nigerian civil servant in this day and age to be willing to help somebody who practically walked off the street into his office. There must be something in it for him or else he would simply dismiss your request out of hand. Then, you are not just ready to accept that those people in Lagos are always on the lookout for themselves and themselves alone. They are dangerous sharks, forever cruising at speed, looking for likely victims. Mark my words, you are going to feel that man's teeth on your tender parts quite soon.'

'You really don't like Lagos and Lagosians' commented Tope.

'You had better believe it, I don't, and with good reason. I lived in Lagos for more than twenty years and I know that the danger lurking on every street corner there is very real.'

'Surely, not all Lagosians are bad' argued one of his hearers.

'I did not say that they were all bad. I just want you to appreciate that you are not likely to ever run into anybody who is willing to give you gratuitous help in Lagos.'

Tope went back to the ministry on the appointed day and his heart very nearly stopped when he was told that in spite of their arrangement, Dr Cole had travelled up to Abuja. Tope, with Eddy's voice ringing in his ears was reassured by Dr Cole's charming secretary that her boss had gone to Abuja to arrange for the release of departmental funds. Tope was immediately elated by this item of intelligence and his elation was complete when he was further informed that Dr Cole had left a telephone number through which he could be contacted. Tope immediately suggested that they called Dr Cole at once.

Unfortunately however, they could not get through to him. This failure cooled Tope's elation, but he was advised to have patience and wait until 2 o'clock in the afternoon when Dr Cole was going to call through to the office.

'We are expecting a message from Dr Cole's son in London and Dr Cole will call to find out if the message has arrived' explained Dr Cole's secretary who then went on to suggest that Tope should wait until then to talk to Dr Cole. This suggestion was immediately accepted by the hopeful supplicant. It was only 11 o'clock at the time and the secretary, thinking that Tope would be bored by the long wait in front of him suggested that he could attend to some other business and come back close to the appointed time.

'No. I will wait' was Tope's emphatic response. 'This is the only business I have in Lagos today and besides, I am too wary of the uncertainties of Lagos traffic to think that I would make it back at the time I have to be back. If you don't think that I will be in the way, I will just make myself comfortable in this chair and hope that the call will come in time.'

The wait turned out to be longer than expected, as the call did not come through until just after 3 o'clock. In the end it was a call very well worth waiting for.

'I am still trying to sort things out' explained Dr Cole. 'Unfortunately, the situation is still not resolved but I am quite confident that success is just round the corner. Mind you I have not sorted out everything, but never mind, you are very close to Brazil.'

'Thank you, thank you very much' gushed Tope who somehow still had the presence of mind to remind Dr Cole that time was running out for him and that he had to be in Brazil in another nine days. Also, there was the problem of his visa that was still to be sorted out.

'There should be no problem about that' responded Dr Cole very calmly. 'We should be able to work something out for you in another three or four days and getting a visa will take only a couple of days since your papers are in order. Don't worry. Everything should be all right.'

'And when should I come back?' asked Tope, the turmoil in his head having been stilled by Dr Cole's calm reassurances.

'I don't want you making unnecessary journeys on those dangerous roads so, why don't you come back say, two days before you are expected to travel. You should come down prepared to travel and we would put you in our Guest-house in Obalende. As for your visa, don't even give it a thought. I can get one of our protocol officers to get it for you, within twenty-four hours, if necessary.'

Tope was fairly dancing with excitement. He had not been told categorically that the desired sponsorship had been granted, but the whole tone of the conversation suggested very broadly that it was as good as in the bag.

The journey back home was most pleasant. As was Tope's wont, he took the opportunity of being alone in the car to muse over a wide variety of topics. His head was full of plans for the coming trip but after about sixty kilometres, his mind began to wander into other regions. When Dr Cole became the subject of attention, his thinking apparatus shifted to a higher gear.

The first thing that came to Tope's mind concerning Dr Cole was that initially, the older man did not make a favourable impression on him. He had classified him as a smooth operator, a man who lacking in substance had sought to overwhelm the senses with appearances. He had come to terms with the thinking that the real source of this initial antipathy was his realisation that unless he had a very strong source of independent income, there was no way that he could finance his standard of living. Besides, he was an inveterate name-dropper and if he was intimate with only half of the number of people he claimed to be friendly with, then he was a man who moved in the highest circle of society. Tope had been intrigued to learn from Dr Cole's secretary that he had two children studying in Britain.

British, or indeed any kind of education is very expensive and when a civil servant on a salary which was only a shade higher than what a lecturer of Tope's grade earned is able to sustain two children in British universities, there was room for a great deal of explanation. It was a simple problem of arithmetic. It should not be possible for a man who earned some ₦40,000 per annum to be able to send two children to Britain when each of them presented a bill running into ₦1 million in the same period of time. How could he do this? Tope shook his head as if to make it work better, but he was still as puzzled as before. Unless of course, he was to admit that the man had his hand buried in the till. It just did not make sense that a man who earned so little could be put in charge of millions of Naira in a country in which accountability was as foreign as a visitor from Mars. If he could bribe his friends in the Treasury with millions of Naira, he could just as well divert even more millions into his own cavernous pockets. On the other hand, that the man was now trying very hard to help him was undeniable and because of this, he was strongly persuaded to reverse his previous judgment, but it has to be said, with great difficulty. These doubts were still worrying him as he drove into the hospital premises to bring his colleagues up to date about the Brazil affair as they had taken to calling it.

Those who were privileged to hear the latest episode in this drama were sure that Tope was on his way to Brazil at last. Since Eddy was not one of these, there was nobody to pour cold water on their premature celebrations. They all competed with each other to shower praise on the absent Dr Cole. As far as they were concerned he represented the best that their profession could offer and wished fervently that there were many more like him.

For the next week, Tope was treading on air. He had rushed around to secure permission to be away from work and also, to travel out of the country. For these, he sent a letter through his Head of Department to the Vice-Chancellor who, noting that the trip was not going to cost the university any money quickly gave his approval. He made sure that he did all that was expected of him by the university and went around making sure that he had everything that he needed for the trip.

The interest generated by Tope's impending trip among the doctors was so great that even though he was going to be away for only six weeks, he was given a rousing send-off. The occasion was particularly enjoyable because the person being sent off bought all the drinks. Some wag calculated that all Tope had to spend to get all of them as drunk as lords was the miserly sum of $15 which he could very well afford to spend since hundreds of dollars were waiting for him across the Atlantic, in Brazil.

Tope left for Lagos in very high spirits and being assured of a warm welcome, he checked into the Ministry of Health Guest-house as he had been told to do by his generous benefactor. He had only two days within which to secure his visa but he was not unduly anxious about this. After all, the protocol officer who was supposed to lead him through the thickets of visa procurement could be relied on to bring him through it all, safe and sound. As for the issue of sponsorship, it did not cross his mind that for one wild moment there could be a slip. As far as he was concerned, the distance between the cup of sponsorship and his lips was so small that the possibility of a mishap was far too remote to be worthy of any serious contemplation.

Early the next morning, which was the day before his scheduled departure, Tope made a leisurely trip to the Ministry of Health. By this time he was such a regular caller that two of the porters recognised him as soon as he presented himself before them and threw him a very sharp salute which he acknowledged with a cheery wave. He sauntered, rather than walked down the corridors to Dr Cole's office where he confidently expected to be received by the secretary and the big boss as well.

In the case of the secretary, Tope's hopes were amply fulfilled as she broke into a dazzling smile as soon as he stepped into the office.

'Good-morning, Doctor' she beamed at a delighted Tope who was further delighted to learn that he was expected.

'Good-morning' replied Tope no less enthusiastically. 'I won't bother to ask how you are because I can see that you are in very fine form,' he went on.

'Ah, Doctor, you are just teasing me' she replied, clearly pleased.

'No, not at all,' protested Tope gallantly. 'You really do brighten up the place. Now can I see Dr Cole?' he asked, getting down to business.

'I am afraid Dr Cole is not in the office. He has travelled out of the country.'

Tope could not believe his ears and he had to take a firm grip of himself before he could manage to ask where Dr Cole had gone.

'He has travelled to Algiers with our minister. I am surprised that he did not tell you about it. It must have slipped his mind. In any case, he has left a letter for you' she said as she handed him an envelope addressed to him in Dr Cole's distinctive handwriting.

'Thank you' said a much-relieved Tope thinking that the letter contained last minute instructions as to how to go about getting his visa and subsequent journey to Rio. Feverish with anticipation, he tore open the letter and went faint with shock, indignation and deep disappointment when the words, "regret, was not able to push through your application" leapt at him from the page. That, as the saying goes, was that!

Life goes on for everyone regardless of circumstances and this is what happened in this case for Tope. His great disappointment was the subject of many heated discussions in the air-conditioned comfort of the Doctors' Room. His colleagues were no less shocked than he was and all of them tried to cheer him up as best as they could. Eventually, in the midst of all the hustle of their professional life, the Brazil affair gradually faded from their collective consciousness. Within two weeks it had become part of the memory, something which may lie there undisturbed for years until it was dusted off and aired as part of a lesson, or even for frivolous entertainment.

The Brazil episode had to all intents and purposes been forgotten when one rainy afternoon, the peace of the Doctors' Room was once again shattered by a whoop of indignation and a volley of ripe oaths from a visibly agitated Tope. As on the previous occasion, these reactions were provoked by a letter, which again bore a brace of foreign stamps.

'Oh, the bastard, the thieving bastard' yelled Tope, just as the others thought that he was sufficiently calm to give them an explanation for his strange behaviour. He was about to launch into another round of incoherence when Bisi asked him to calm down and explain why he was in such a state. Tope did not answer but thrust the offending missive into his hand.

Bisi read it and whistled very loudly.

'Why!' he shouted angrily, 'this man should be in jail. How could he have done such a thing!'

Finally, he got a grip on himself and read the letter to the others who by then were dying to know the cause of the disturbance. The letter was supposed to have been written in English, but it was peppered with so many Portuguese words and others which sounded like French that it was rather like a jig-saw puzzle, to be put together with skill in order that it could be comprehensible. The summary was however very plain. It was written by a lady called Ritta. She lived in Rio de Janeiro and had written to remind Tope of the wonderful time that they had spent together during his recent visit to Rio. According to her, she was very much looking forward to an opportunity for them to renew their acquaintanceship and do more of those things which they had so enjoyed doing together.

Enclosed with the letter was a picture of the stunningly beautiful Ritta, dancing cheek to cheek with an obviously ecstatic Dr Cole, in a Rio night-club.

I don't believe it. I can't believe it. It really is impossible for me to believe that I am actually sitting down and without coercion, writing these lines. I am simply not the writing kind and cannot remember any precedence to this instance. When I was in school, the secondary school that is, I struggled to write essays on all sorts of subjects chosen, as I thought, with fiendish delight by teachers who were at least slightly demented. I never managed to impress any of them and as soon as I passed out of their hands, I hung up my pen for good. I have to do a bit of writing in my line of business, but all that writing is of a technical nature requiring not a jot of imagination. This is not to say that I have no imagination. Indeed my mind is fairly seething with all manner of exciting ideas. It is just that I cannot, for the life of me, think and write at the same time. Why not think first and write later, you may ask. I don't know and that is the simple truth.

That I am writing these lines is testimony to my desperation. I don't know how that strikes you because you may think that writing is a sign of desperation whereas all I mean is that I am desperate and therefore I write. I write in the hope that by writing, I may find a way out of the mental maze in which I have been wandering for months now.

I have confessed my inability to write so I have prepared the ground for another confession. I find reading painfully boring. My acquaintance with books has been like my writing, severely restricted to technical literature and a newspaper every now and then. My recreational activities are decidedly non-cerebral and if I were to tell the truth, not athletic either unless you stretch athletics to include sex. Plain, old-fashioned sex, with a willing companion in the missionary position. It would be unfair however to categorise me as being obsessed with sex. Or maybe, I should just say that I am no more obsessed with this subject than any other full-blooded male of my acquaintance. Yes, I think that is the safest way of describing my attitude to sex, which I have heard, described by people far more knowledgeable than I, as man's most basic instinct.

This is however not a treatise on sex. I am not qualified to attempt to do something so academic. As I said at the outset, I very much doubt my ability to write at all and in any case I cannot describe my current activity as writing, since that supposes that my effort will be read by anyone else. If I thought that this piece of writing would be read by anyone else at any time in the future, I would not have come to the point of actually putting pen to paper. This activity is a form of therapy. I have come to the inescapable conclusion that I am battling with forces right outside my control and if I am to grapple successfully with them, I have to come to terms with them. Pin them down so to say and examine them in great detail. Maybe, after that, I would not be so handicapped in dealing with them. So, the primary aim of this "literary effort" is to identify the demons tormenting me and hopefully, exorcise them.

My problem is that I am in the grip of lust, a lust so corrosive that it has banished all thought from my mind and has changed my life drastically. It is a lust that is actually threatening my life. What makes my situation intolerable, is that I am not talking in terms of an urge to indulge in general or random sexual activity. I would have been satisfied a long time ago were this to be so. No. This lust was kindled and stoked by a particular girl until it has become a conflagration that is now threatening to consume me. I don't know where to turn for advice because I have only a few friends and I cannot think of any of them who would dispense any sympathy to me over what they are very likely to regard as being inconsequential. And yet, I feel that I must relieve the pressure, which has built up in my mind by talking about my predicament.

Another reason why I have been reticent about this matter is that I find it acutely embarrassing. How could I, an experienced sampler of flesh be trapped in this way by a mere slip of a girl, the kind of novice that I could have sworn I would have had for breakfast only a few months ago. Yes, I am ashamed to be caught out and not only that, to be frustrated in my corrosive desires.

I have, if I am going to be frank, and I intend to be, never seriously thought that a problem could be half-solved by talking about it to another person. At the same time, I have always remembered a story about a man who reduced the load on his mind by the simple process of translating his thoughts into words. I really don't think that I will allow other eyes other than mine to ever see these lines and so, they are meant to serve one purpose only: catharsis for an overwrought mind. At the same time, there cannot be any harm telling this story, just in case it makes me feel better somehow. I was made to read this story a very long time ago and I am not sure that my memory is correct in every detail, but that can hardly be important. The outline is quite clear to me.

A long time ago... all stories of these nature begin this way, possibly to make corroboration impossible since most of it is pure fiction anyway. In any case, it was a very long time ago that Alade made friends with Kola. They were such firm friends that there was nothing that they did not share with each other. They were like one unit, doing everything and going everywhere together. There was nothing about Kola that Alade did not know and there was nothing about Alade that Kola did not know, except for one thing that is. Alade went everywhere with a heavily embroidered cap on his head. The cap fitted so tightly that it was nearly taken to be part of Alade's head. From time to time, it crossed Kola's mind to ask his friend why he was never without his cap, even in bed, but each time that this temptation intruded into his thoughts, he resisted it stoutly. He was willing to wait until Alade let him into the secret of his famous cap. His reasoning was that there had to be a secret or else, he would have been put in the picture a long time before then.

In the matter of being enlightened without prompting, Kola was under an illusion, as Alade remained resolutely silent. In the end, Kola could no longer resist the temptation to know, and he finally put the question to his friend.

'Alade', Kola solemnly called his friend on that fateful day. 'You know that we have been friends who have shared everything. You know all that is to know about me, but I cannot say the same about you.'

At this point, Kola looked at his friend full in the face as if to read it like a book. After a full minute, he continued rather hesitantly, not quite sure how his inquiries would be received as Alade's face had become inscrutable.

'Well, you see, I have often wondered why you are never without that cap on your head' he blurted out finally.

Alade's response was silence, a brooding, unhealthy silence, which could be a prelude to just about anything. Kola was understandably anxious about how the silence would be broken, but he waited patiently for his friend to say something.

At last Alade broke the silence with a heavy sigh, a sound which seemed to have had its origins in the pit of his stomach, so heavy was it when it dropped from his lips.

'Humph, my friend, my dear friend, I have often wondered when you would ask me this question. I am even surprised that you have not asked it much earlier. After all it is certainly strange for anyone to have a cap on his head all the time. I would in fact have told you about my problem long before now, but I did not want you to carry this burden which has been mine to carry for quite some time now.'

With that, he removed his cap with a sad flourish and, sticking out of his head like a goat's was a horn!

Kola, poor, poor Kola let out a gasp of horror and pity.

'I had no idea' he stammered. 'I would never have been able to guess correctly why you always wore a cap, but now that I know, I give you my solemn promise that I will forever keep your secret to myself.'

'I am very sorry to have doubted your discretion in this matter' Alade said as he clasped Kola to his bosom.

Kola made a promise and he was determined to keep it, come hell or high water. Unfortunately, human affairs are marked neither by hell nor high water. Being a human being, he was subject to mental pressures, which he did not even know about. From that fateful day on, he woke up with Alade's secret on the tip of his tongue and from that minute, battled hard to ensure that it did not tumble off his tongue into some ear conveniently placed to catch it. Soon, the strain began to show as he grew increasingly taciturn and began to lose weight. His appetite, which until then had been remarkably healthy, began to wane alarmingly and his sleep became increasingly disturbed. Kola's condition became a source of worry and even alarm to Alade who could not help but notice his friend's precipitous decline. His fear was that his friend had become the victim of some obscure but virulent organic disease.

On his part, Kola did not for one moment doubt that his condition was brought on by the piece of intelligence which he had more or less forced out of his friend and which having swallowed, he could not bring up again. The existence of a horn on Alade's head was killing him literally and short of betraying his friend, there was nothing he could do about it. After a great deal of thought, he decided to seek expert opinion from the local medicine-man (or doctor), a wily old fellow who ministered to the mental, physical and spiritual needs of a large clientele since he was also a priest.

Kola went for consultation one evening dragging an understandably reluctant goat with which to pay the doctor's consultation fees. The goat was tied to a convenient post outside the doctor's clinic and Kola went straight into the consulting room in which the doctor/priest sat on a reed mat, deep in meditation.

The first ten minutes, or so were taken up with elaborate greetings as the consultant asked after every member of Kola's extended family, all of whom he knew quite well. It was after all the formalities had been got out of the way that Kola broached the subject of his visit. In doing so however, he was very careful not to give away Alade's secret, so that the route along which the doctor was taken on this particular journey was by necessity, long-winding. His hearer was fortunately very experienced in such matters and listened most attentively and without any undue interruption.

'Well', began Kola, clearing his throat quite dramatically but unnecessarily, 'I have a very delicate problem.'

'Umm' was the doctor's sympathetic response.

'As you must have noticed, I am losing a lot of weight. My sleep has been very much disturbed and my appetite has deserted me. In short, I can no longer enjoy life and I am becoming quite desperate about this unwelcome development.'

'For how long have you been feeling this way?' the doctor asked.

'Oh, it has been going on for a couple of months now. I know because it was around the time that I planted my crop of maize. Incidentally, that crop has been a source of considerable worry to me on account of the lateness of the rains this year.'

'Are you sure that your maize and other crops are not contributing to what ails you at this time?' asked the doctor.

'No. I don't think so' responded Kola very firmly. 'Worrying about the state of crops is a permanent feature of a farmer's life. I doubt very much that this will prey on my mind to such an extent that it would blight my existence in the way that this problem has done.'

'In a case like this, every aspect of the situation must be examined carefully. Nothing must be overlooked as the success of any intervention will depend on every little detail' explained the doctor.

'I quite appreciate the importance of supplying all the information I have about this condition,' the doctor was assured, 'and I think that I will only be making matters as clear as they can be when I say that my friend is behind all these.'

The doctor who had been expecting something of this nature was not in the least surprised that Kola suspected that someone was responsible for his condition. Indeed, it would have been contrary to his expectation had Kola not suspected that he was the victim of the evil machinations of someone very close to him.

'Why do you think that your friend is responsible for your trouble? Is there some disagreement between the two of you? Are you aware of any reason whatsoever why your friend, or anyone else for that matter may be after you?' The questions came thick and fast.

'Oh! I don't mean that my friend has cast a spell on me, or done any other such thing as may cause me harm' explained Kola.

'What exactly do you mean?' was the next query.

Kola was not quite clear in his mind how to proceed without jeopardising Alade's secret, but in the end, he was persuaded to tell all, at least, very nearly all.

'It is like this. My very close friend has entrusted a very delicate secret to me. Even before admitting me to this secret, I swore never to divulge it to anybody under any imaginable circumstance and I intend to keep this promise at all costs. It is just that ever since he gave me this piece of information, I have been under tremendous pressure to pass it on to somebody else and what more, this pressure has increased day after day until now, it is threatening to blow me apart. Any time that I meet anybody along the way, I am tempted, very sorely tempted to call him aside and whisper what my friend told me in his ears. I have to keep a tight hold of myself whenever I go to the market because of the nearly irresistible urge I have to make an announcement concerning my friend to everybody in the market. I am forever thinking about this item of information and the fear that I will not be able to hold on for much longer is growing stronger by the day. I need help and I need it now!' concluded Kola, his voice fairly breaking with emotion.

'This is certainly a very strange case, but it is not one beyond my competence. I have come across something like it on one or two previous occasions. You need to relieve your mind of the heavy load, which at the moment is weighing it down. At the same time, you must not betray your friend.'

'How can that be done?' cried Kola in considerable alarm.

'Oh, it is not as difficult as you think' came the calm reassurance.

'You can satisfy your urge to tell it all by going right outside of town, digging a hole into which you will shout your friend's secret and covering it up again, to seal in your words forever. Whenever the urge becomes irresistible, you must repeat this exercise until such a time, as you will be cured completely.'

This was one treatment schedule that Kola was determined to comply with, and what more, he made up his mind to proceed right away. He left the doctor's clinic and headed straight out of town until he came to a place, which was completely deserted. There, he dug a hole, knelt down and with his mouth inside it, shouted, 'Alade has a horn on his head.' He looked around to reassure himself that there was nobody within earshot before filling in the hole as he had been asked to do. He needed to do this on a few more occasions before he was able to declare that he had been cured. End of story? Not quite.

By the next rainy season, some children noticed that some reeds were growing around the area where Kola had "planted" Alade's secret. These reeds were of the kind from which the children could fashion out a rough flute and soon they were making and blowing these flutes. The first boy to make a flute from one of these reeds could hardly believe his ears when he blew into his toy and out came the message in clear tones, "Alade has a horn on his head". Alade's secret was thereby revealed to all those who had ears to hear the message which virtually all the boys in town were spreading all over the town.

For every secret that is committed to paper or vocalised in any way, there are reed flutes, which will ensure that the secret becomes public at one time or the other so, I am well-aware of the risk I am running, but I really cannot help myself. I must write. It is now not so much that in writing I may find relief any more. It is that I am now committed to putting my tortures down on paper. As for the risk of eventual discovery, so what? It is said that it is to frighten the person concerned in a particular matter that people say that such a thing had never been known to happen before. So what is new, especially in the area of human sexuality? Is my story any stranger than many of those reported in newspapers?

My troubles began just over a month ago. It had been a very hot and muggy day and I was making my way home through town in my battered old car, thinking initially of a cool bath, a light supper and a spot of matrimonial sex. Soon however, it was only the sex on my mind and even the complexion of that changed from the sedate roll around with the wife to something wild and strange, a romp through uncharted territory. My mind was thus occupied when I arrived at the busiest road junction in town. There, I had to wait for a large articulated lorry, which did not have the right of way, but had seized it anyway, to be manoeuvred past a mini-bus, which had been ill-advisedly abandoned by the roadside. It was while I was thus immobilised that I saw this young lady standing on the other side of the road from me. She might have been waiting for a taxi, a lover or her father. I did not stop to think, but beckoned to her as at that moment, our eyes met across the road.

My signal to the young lady was more hesitant than authoritative and I really did not think that I would get any kind of response. I was wrong. Her hesitation was for a brief moment, then her face was lit up by a big grin, one so warm that initially, I did not think that it was meant for me. I was wrong again. The grin was for my benefit. Further to that, she crossed the street over to me and got into the car without any prompting.

I looked across at my totally unexpected guest and although I had made the first move, I was quite unable to think of an appropriate response to this gorgeous creature who had dropped into my lap from goodness knows where. Fortunately I had the presence of mind to look round me and found that the obstruction which had halted my progress had been cleared and I was therefore able to move once again. I betrayed my agitation by treading too hard on the accelerator so that the car jerked forward as if a giant hand had roughly shoved it. The vehicle leapt forward, narrowly missing the car in front, before rocking back as I took my foot off the offending pedal.

'Sorry' I murmured to my passenger who just smiled by way of an answer. To tell the truth I had no idea how to proceed from that point without sounding like a fool and I did not want to give the young lady the impression that I was not all there. I thought of telling her that she looked familiar, but discarded that notion. It was such a common ploy in such circumstances that I thought it unworthy of a grown man like me.

'Where are you going?' I found myself asking her at last.

'Orile' was the one-word response.

'Orile is a long way from here, so what is taking you all the way there at this time of the day?'

'I am going there to see my auntie' she replied.

'You must really love your auntie to go all that way' I said.

'Oh it is not so far from here and her husband can take me back home in his car. He has a new car, you know.'

I thought I could detect a hint of sarcasm in her tone, but I quickly dismissed this as being more imagined than real, a feeling brought on by the fact that my own car had been brand new, a little over twenty years before.

'It is good to have a rich in-law, but we are going in the opposite direction to your destination' I pointed out to her.

'That's all right, I am not in any great hurry' she assured me.

'In that case, you can come with me?'

'And where is it that you are going?' she asked.

I could not tell her that I had been on my way home before I met her and in any case, the thought of home had been driven clean out of my mind, the moment I saw her. So, I wasn't fibbing when I told her that I was on my way to see a friend of mine. The fellow I had in mind, was Leke who at that point in time was a bachelor, his wife, Kemi having gone off to Liverpool to "look for something to eat" as she put it. Kemi and Leke had been battling with problems of a financial nature for a couple of years and in the end, resolved that the only way out of their predicament was for Kemi to go back to England where she had obtained her nursing qualification almost twenty years before. She was to earn pounds sterling which when converted into the nearly valueless naira would translate into a small fortune with which to take care of their myriad responsibilities. Leke, being broad-minded and not above the kind of peccadilloes which I had in mind, would certainly not mind his flat being used as a love-nest by my lovely catch and I. But, the lady had other ideas.

'I certainly will not go to your friend's house with you' she said, the note of finality in her voice clearly unmistakable.

'Why not?' I asked. 'Leke will be happy to see you' I tried to assure her.

'He may be happy to see me, but what about his wife?'

'His wife? Did I say anything about his wife?' His wife, if you must know, will not be there to meet you. She is in Liverpool.'

'I don't care where she is' she replied. 'I refuse to go into a married man's home.' Her tone brooked no further argument.

'Where do we go then?' I asked in considerable agitation, not to say irritation. After all, I was an unmistakably married man and she was willing to go places with me.

'Oh, anywhere else you wish to go' she said airily, as if she did not care one way or the other, as long as it was not to Leke's house and the soft double bed in his guest-room, which was the destination I had in mind.

'That is not a helpful answer' my irritation deepening. 'You turned down my perfectly good suggestion and now it is your turn to tell us where you want us to go' I concluded rather sulkily.

She just laughed. The laughter bubbled out of her and melted my irritation clean away.

'Men!' she said in a bantering tone. 'Ten minutes ago you did not know that I existed and just because I got in your car, you think that you can do what you want with me. Right now, you have only one thing on your mind and that is to get me into bed with you. Just like that!' she concluded with a snap of her fingers.

I had no answer to this and decided to keep my peace. After all, my passenger was quite right about everything. I just sat there trying not to look hurt, but not succeeding.

After a few minutes of charged silence, I got the bright idea of steering her to what can be said to be neutral ground by asking her for her name, which she informed me was Titi Ojo.

'What do you do for a living?' I asked her further.

'Nothing' was her prompt response.

'What do you mean, nothing? Surely, you don't sit at home all day twiddling your thumbs, or doing something just as useless' I told her.

'When I said nothing, I meant nothing' she responded with considerable heat. 'I don't do anything as you put it because I have just passed out of the secondary school and I am waiting to go into the university.'

'I see' I said, not seeing anything at all, but thinking furiously what to do next. Then she came to my rescue by saying that she wanted a drink of palm-wine from a place just outside town.

'I don't remember what we talked about as we travelled towards the palm-wine that she wanted. She kept looking at me as if she was trying to make up her mind about something concerning me, or maybe that was just my fancy.

I am not a palm-wine drinker, but because that was what she wanted, I took some too and as we drank, I got more sexually aroused and I was sure so did she. She was not just smiling in my face but was stroking my arms and rubbing against me in the manner of an amorous cat. I was under her spell right from the beginning, but now I was her willing slave, ready to risk my life if necessary, to make love to her. I became blind and deaf to everything around me and allowed myself to be sucked into her. In other words, 1 was just a body, an empty shell prepared to be used in the service of my mistress.

By the time she was ready to head back to the town, I was a lost soul, just dying to lay my hands on her. Apparently she was just as ready for sex as I was because no sooner did we get into the car than she had her hands on my crotch and began to do some unbelievable things to me.

'Do you want to get us killed?' I asked in a strangled voice.

'No' she replied huskily. 'Just stop the car and I will show you something.'

I did as I was told and she got out of the car and started walking into the bush at the side of the road. As she disappeared from view, she turned round to me and beckoned imperiously for me to follow. I obeyed her instantly and no sooner were we in the shade of the cocoa trees in a farm very nearby, did she turn to me, locking me in the most delicious embrace I had ever been subjected to in my life. I had no time to contemplate this because she was kissing me not just on the mouth but all over, her tongue flicking in and out of places where I had never been kissed before. In this encounter, Titi was the aggressor, initiating moves, which until then I thought were reserved for the male of the species. I was fairly swooning with the headiness of it all and I distinctly felt the earth move beneath us as she divested me of my clothing and gave herself to me like a sacrifice to the god of love. There, on our surprisingly comfortable bed of leaves we made love with joyous abandon, both of us reaching several climaxes, each one more glorious than the last. Even as I lay there trying to regain my breath and fearing that I had done myself some grievous and permanent injury, I wondered how it was that so much passion could be locked up in the slight body lying beside me. It was the most memorable experience of that kind that I had ever had and I knew there and then, that I was lost, hooked as securely as an addict to some potent and dangerous drug.

It was nearly dark by the time we came back to earth and made our way back to town. It was of course too late for Titi to go and see her auntie that day and all that was on my mind was when I would get to see her again.

'When are we two going to meet again?' I asked her, my body already showing signs of recovery from the gross abuse to which it had recently been subjected.

'Soon,' she said, 'we must meet very soon!' her eyes sparkling in that special way that betrays sexual satisfaction.

'Do you think tomorrow will be soon enough?' I asked in a rather lordly manner, confident that I was in control.

'Tomorrow will be fine' she said as I thought she would. 'Let us meet at the junction from where you picked me up today and we can go and drink some more palm-wine' she concluded, with a roguish smile on her face.

'I will be there at 5 o'clock sharp, but what of if you are not there?'

'I will be there' she assured me.

'I don't want to take chances and I think you should give me your address so that if I miss you, I will know where to come looking for you.'

'I have no address' she replied.

'What do you mean you have no address? You must live somewhere.'

'I live in a house in our family compound and you should know that such places are not numbered. We don't even have proper streets in my part of town but if you must know, I live in Eleko's compound, but don't worry, I will be at our junction on time tomorrow.'

I drove away from her in a daze and I was already back home before my thoughts were switched away from the incredibly passionate body of Titi Ojo. My mind might have been rescued from Titi's body, but my body was not. It was still tingling as I got into the house and called out a careless greeting to my wife who was busy in the kitchen preparing supper. I did not want to talk to anybody at that time so I made straight for the bathroom more to prevent human contact of any kind than in making use of the sanitary facilities there.

*   *   *   *   *

I cannot tell you how the following day went. Every passing moment was important only because it brought me closer to the magical hour of 5 o'clock and the exquisite delights of Titi Ojo. I could not concentrate on any tasks because there was just no room in my head for anything outside the expectation of the sexual delights that I was sure were coming with the appointed hour. I was at the stipulated junction in plenty of time for our meeting and waited impatiently for Titi to appear. I waited in vain. After waiting for half an hour, the awful suspicion that she was not coming stole into my mind and I began to fear the worst. After one hour, I knew that she was not coming and I began my search for Eleko's compound. It was not easy.

Off the busy streets, a maze of paths snaked between houses, which had stood shoulder to shoulder for several decades, creating many towns within the town. These towns existed without any discernible landmarks to the uninitiated such as I was. I asked for directions from passers-by, but the more directions I got, the more confused I became. I found myself stumbling around like a bat, which had lost its radar or a pigeon with its homing device out of commission. I was well and truly lost in a town, which I fancied I knew very well. In desperation, I stumbled into a bar, a place in which I might find a mellow spirit who would solve my problem. I was right. The first man I talked to not only knew the neighbourhood like the back of his hand, but was willing to take me right to the door of my destination. After all, according to him, it was just around the corner. And so it was.

The Eleko compound was a replica of that crazy, jumbled-up neighbourhood. It was made of sets of rooms and passages, which to my eyes looked incredibly unwieldy. One way of describing the place is to say that should a thief stray into that compound, he is likely to continue to look for a way out until he drops from exhaustion. No thief would of course even dream of breaking into the place after dar'. as he would have had to break out again, a wiser and more careful thief than he went in.

I had not come to steal but my manner could not have been more furtive if I had. I would have been very comfortable had I come to a conventional house with rooms, which could be recognised as such. In this strange collection of rooms and passages, nothing looked like anything I had ever encountered before. People passed in and out of what I took to be the main entrance rather like ants scurrying in and out of their holes each one hell-bent on completing some esoteric but vital task. It therefore took me some time to identify a person from whom I could make inquiries about Titi.

The person I hit upon to give me information was an old man in a rocking chair placed in one of the passages close to the main entrance. I thought that an old-timer like him was sure to know most, if not all the people who lived in that compound.

'Good-evening sir' I greeted him with as much reverence as I could muster.

'Good-evening' he responded but without the warmth that I expected from him.

'Sir' I pressed on regardless, 'I am looking for Titi Ojo. Could you tell me how I could find her?'

My first impression was that he had not heard my request because he made no response for a longish period.

'Did you say Titi Ojo?' he asked, just when I thought I should put my question to him again.

'Yes sir' I responded.

'And who are you, where are you from?' the old man queried.

I did not think that I might be called upon to provide answers to questions like these and so I was rather startled by this interrogation.

Who was I? The honest response would have been that I was a randy old so and so who wished to be serviced by the passionate Titi. This was an answer I could very well not give since it might have upset the old man who for all I knew was Titi's father, or rather grandfather. I took refuge in a lie.

'I am a teacher in her old school and I have come in respect of some books which Titi borrowed from me when she was a student and forgot to return before she left school.'

As far as I could judge, my story had not made any impression on the old man.

'That is all right' he said, 'except that nobody called Titi Ojo lives in this compound.'

'Are you sure about that sir?' I asked, with just a hint of a snap to my question.

'Of course I am sure. I know everybody in this compound and take it from me, there is nobody by that name here.'

'I see' I said, not seeing at all.

'Thank you very much sir' I said as I turned to go. I was dazed with disappointment.

Each day for the next week, I went all over town looking for Titi. I went from stall to stall in the main market and drew a blank each time. I went round to all the schools in the neighbourhood and did not catch even a glimpse of her. I made inquiries about her at the palm-wine bar where we had taken palm-wine together but nobody could make any response to my questions. Apparently, Titi had not been in there on any occasion previous to our joint visit to the place. I went round to all public places and in each case drew a blank. It was as if Titi had simply disappeared without trace. Commonsense dictated that I put Titi out of my mind but my unreflective body willed otherwise. I simply had to find Titi! Failure in this respect did not discourage me. It only made me more determined to find Titi, come what may.

For a whole month, I searched most diligently for Titi to the exclusion of all other things. It seemed that I lived only to look for this girl who after some time, I suddenly realised, I may not even recognise if I saw her. It was then that it dawned on me that Titi had become super-human. She had become an obsession. And yet, I could not even think of giving up and not only that I could not ask anyone for advice.

After a time, I began to ask if Titi was real. After all, my overwrought mind was beginning to ask for proof of her existence. And that was when my troubles really began. If Titi was not real, who was it that I made love to in that cocoa farm? Nothing could be more real than that and I had the evidence of my memory to support the fact of Titi's corporeal existence, only I could not find her to prove that existence.

My every waking moment was devoted to Titi. This was bad enough but what was to follow was worse, much worse. My sleeping moments, such as they were, were soon invaded by this elusive creature. I began to see her in my dreams, which soon took on the quality of nightmares. At the beginning, I saw her as a fresh, young lady, which was how I remembered her, smiling seductively, again, as I remembered that she did. Soon, she looked like a very tired middle-aged woman, hair greying, cheeks collapsing, wrinkles threading their way across her once delightful features. In the next few nights she had moved on to advanced old age, her hands shaped like claws, her grin hideous with malice and the few strands of hair left to her, white with age. And yet she was unmistakably Titi, at least as far as my overworked imagination was concerned. What really turned my dreams into nightmares was that I was still trying to make love to the hideous crone, which visited my bed every night, just as I tried to do when she was young and fresh, pulsing with the warm juices of irrepressible youth.

My sleep, having been invaded by this apparition, became a form of torture. I was burning up with desire day and night, and yet, I was as limp as a wet rag in the presence of other women, one of who was as willing as any women could be. I had been a dutiful if not overly passionate lover to my wife. In the strange condition in which I found myself however, I just could not find the will to do anything sexual with her, let alone satisfy her needs in this direction. Fortunately, because I was so obviously listless and losing weight, she thought that I was suffering with some wasting disease and insisted that I saw a doctor.

I complied with her wishes and described my symptoms, such as they were to the doctor, a harassed man with too much to do and too little to do them with. He could not be bothered with a man whose tests showed that he was perfectly normal. So, he loaded me down with sleeping tablets and as many vitamin preparations as were available in the hospital pharmacy. I did not get better. The sleeping pills only improved the bizarre quality of my dreams and pumped up the horror of my nightly trips to the land of dreams, from where I returned panting and sweating.

My condition did not improve even when for some inexplicable reason, the old crone of my dreams was suddenly transformed into a beautiful girl once more. At that point, it seemed that the horror had been taken out of my life.

'Titi!' I cried when this happened, 'where have you been all these days?'

'Here by your side, my dear' she replied with a smile which caused my heart to race.

'I have missed you terribly!' I cried plaintively. 'Some broken down old woman has been pretending to be you and was driving me insane.'

She did not give an answer to this but continued to smile sweetly.

'In any case I am happy now that you are back.'

'But you silly man' she insisted, 'I have always been here with you and wouldn't dream of leaving your side for as much as one minute.'

'If you have been here with me all the time, then that old witch scaring me to death was you, and there is no way I can believe that.'

'Okay, believe what you want, the important thing is that I am here with you, so think of the present and the moments we will spend together. Forget the past if it is too distressing' she advised.

'How can I forget the past?' I cried. 'I have been here with some loathsome hag, consumed with passion for you and now that you are here, you say I should forget the past, just like that!' I snapped my fingers, as I remembered she did on that fateful day of our meeting.

That snap launched me out of sleep, but for once I was not too distressed. Titi was back and looking friendly, so things were looking up. There was hope for me yet, I thought. True she was not there in the flesh, nevertheless we could now meet, even if it was only in dreamland.

My mood improved that day and for the first time, in a long while, I perked up quite a bit and I recovered part of the appetite for food, which I had lost. By this time, I had given up my physical search for Titi if only because I had already gone through the town with a fine-toothed comb and was convinced that there was no way I could have missed her if she was anywhere in that locality. True, I was always ready for meeting up with her but this was more as a sop to my raging desire rather than any hope of fulfilment.

The night following that good day was even better. Titi came again and this time, there was no mistaking her friendliness. Not only was her greeting warm, she stroked my face, drawing her fingers across my brow in a gesture of great tenderness. I was in ecstasy. I looked into her face as if to memorise her features. Her eyes held mine captive, those eyes, which were like deep pools into which my whole being was plunged. I lost myself in her all over again.

Titi had come to me made up like a woman visiting a much-cherished lover. Her hair had been braided into hundreds of thin plaits, which fell over her face like a waterfall, a cascade of blackness, captivating and tantalising the senses. Some beads had been braided into her coiffure, which sparkled in a delightful riot of colours. Her full lips were painted cherry red and looked incredibly sexy, the kind of lips, luscious in their ripeness which could bring life to the most tired of jaded loins. They certainly kicked mine to life. Her soft fingers, long, slim and tapering at the tips moved over my face, her touch as soft and silky as a spider's web, setting my whole body on fire.

'Titi! Titi!' I murmured over and over again stringing my utterance together until it sounded like an incantation which was to serve as an evocation of all the amatory spirits that dwelt in the subject of my adoration.

'Titi! Titi!' I chanted on and on, unable to think of anything else to say. Then it occurred to me to tell her that I missed her and so the quality of my chant changed and told the lady how much I missed her and begged piteously that she should never leave me.

'Oh, you silly man' she sighed, 'why do you insist that I left you when I have always been by your side?'

'How is it that I did not feel your presence then?' I cried.

'That is only because you do not love me' she replied, the sadness in her voice poignant and unmistakable.

I was shocked, shocked to the very marrow of my bones. Did I hear right? How could Titi, my enchantress and torturer talk about love?

To tell the truth, I had never, up till that moment associated Titi with love. It came to me in a flash that my mind had been preoccupied with lust, which was not even related to love. Now she was demanding love and I could not help but wonder if I was going to be able to give it to her.

'Love me and we would always be together' Titi promised with impressive solemnity.

'But I love you already' I insisted weakly, knowing that my assertion could not be true. She was not deceived.

'No, you don't!' she said emphatically.

I had no answer to this and she went on.

'You are only pretending to love me, but I know better. All you wish to do is possess me, slake your thirst in my pool and move on to another flower from which to suck more nourishment. What you feel for me is lust and that is not sufficient to satisfy my needs. I need love. I need someone to love me for myself and not for any excitement that I can bring to his life and body.'

This was getting too heavy for me and I said so, but we could not go any further because I woke up at this point, shattering Titi's image into a thousand small fragments and plunging my spirits into an icy sea of depression. At that instant, I was not able to define reality. What I took to be dreams were so real that waking up appeared to be an interruption of reality. What was reality anyway if it excluded Titi? As far as I was concerned, Titi had the substance of reality and so I was conscious only in my dreams which therefore were not dreams but a concrete existence on another plane.

At the time that this writing exercise started, I did not know how serious my condition was. Indeed, I thought that my desire for Titi, as all-consuming as it was, had an element of farce about it and that it could not be more than a passing fancy, an episode to be remembered in the future with much shaking of the head and nothing more. At this point, I was not so sure anymore about what I was dealing with, or perhaps more appropriately, what was dealing with me. I was now badly frightened and considered that it was time to put the case before someone who could give me useful advice before I went off my head, or worse.

The opportunity to do this came sooner than I expected. Some of my friends had noticed the air of abstraction, which had attached itself to me and one of them, Bode, took it upon himself to investigate. He came to me wanting to know what the matter was with me and fortunately his timing was perfect. Had he come only a while earlier, I would have assured him that there was nothing the matter with me, or that I was having a little trouble with my sleep, or some other such trivial worry, not worth bothering about. Now that I thought that I was right out of my depth however, I was more than willing to tell all and I did.

Long after my narration was over, Bode did not utter a word. He just sat there staring at me and trying to disguise the look of alarm, which nevertheless, was spreading across his face.

All he managed to say after a long period of silence and reflection was that I was extremely lucky to be alive.

It was now my turn to be alarmed.

'Lucky to be alive?' I echoed.

'Yes indeed!' Bode affirmed.

'I don't understand you. How did you come to the conclusion that my life has been in danger? I would have thought that there were grounds for entertaining fears about my sanity, but I am sure that my life is as safe as it ever was. Even the doctor who tested me recently could not find anything seriously wrong with me.'

Bode was not impressed and it showed plainly on his expressive face.

'You have been playing a dangerous game even if you did not appreciate what was going on.'

I was more than slightly irritated by the obvious note of certainty in his voice. After all, what could he know about what I had been through, I reasoned.

'And you are sure about what has been happening to me?' was my slightly acid response.

He did not bother to acknowledge my retort.

'Do you believe in ghosts?'

'Ghosts? What have ghosts got to do with what we are talking about?'

'Everything my friend, everything. I am sure that this precious Titi of yours is a ghost.'

'What?' I shouted. 'A ghost is intangible, but let me assure you that this precious Titi of mine as you call her was as solidly physical as you are now. I know. I felt her and having done so, I doubt that I will ever forget her reality.'

'The trouble with you is that you are altogether too physical. Unless you can actually feel something through one or more of your five senses, you cannot conceive of its reality, or its existence. You have therefore imposed a very low limit on your experience of life. The point which you need to appreciate is that there is reality, concrete reality beyond the physical and not until you understand this would you be able to come to terms with what is happening to you.'

'I am afraid, I cannot follow you' I confessed after a few moments of reflection.

'I did not think you would, or could, so just listen to me' advised Bode. 'Titi may have been alive when you met her and I am not willing to bet that she was, but I am quite sure that she is dead as at now. Just listen!' he said as he noticed that I wanted to say something. 'Yes' he continued, 'I am sure that she is dead as this is the only explanation that can support your experience so far. As you conceded, there are other women and yet you appear to be securely tied to this particular woman that you cannot even find. Haven't you at any time suspected that you were in the grip of something beyond your powers, something that can only be described as supernatural?'

'I knew that something beyond the limits of my understanding was happening to me', I confessed, 'but I did not think that it was in any way supernatural' I added.

'You have been lucky. That much I know. There is no doubt that she was not convinced of your love for her otherwise, she would have taken you with her to the other side, the other side being the grave. You have to do something about this situation now before she wins you over and puts you in your grave.'

My first inclination was to scoff at what my friend had said, but on second thoughts, I decided to hear him out. After all, I turned to him out of desperation and respect for his ability to give me useful advice about something, which was clearly beyond me.

'Okay,' I said, 'let us agree that my life is in considerable danger. What do you suppose that I should do to protect myself from succumbing to this pull from beyond the grave?' Even then, I was not sure that all traces of sarcasm had been purged from my tone.

'I am afraid I cannot give you a reliable answer to that question and that is because what we have on our hands here is in my estimation, so deep that I rather think that you should not take any chances. You must take yourself off to see someone who is competent to handle your case and what more, you must do so immediately. There can be no telling when your ghost-wife will claim you for herself.'

I shivered in spite of my scepticism about Bode's analysis of my problem. It may be true that there are no such things as ghosts, in which case, Bode was just blowing a lot of hot air. On the other hand, suppose that Bode was somehow correct in his understanding of the situation? In that case, I would be in considerable danger and should therefore not take any chances.

'Do you know somebody who can be of help?' I asked.

'As a matter of fact, I do.' Bode assured me.

'When do you think we would be able to see your man?'

'You really don't appreciate the danger you are in, do you? Get this very clear. If I were you, I would seek help today. Right away in fact. The man I have in mind lives almost fifty kilometres away in a small village. The road leading to the place is, as you should expect, in poor shape and it will take us nearly two hours to get there in that ancient car of yours. My suggestion is that we drop everything now and try to get to Olotu which is where my man, as you call him, lives.'

By then, I had become thoroughly frightened and was ready to do anything to put the matter right. I had never undertaken the kind of journey which Bode had suggested and all kinds of fantastic images were flashing through my mind. Going to a *Babalawo* as Bode had suggested went so much against the grain of my world view however, that even in that state, a small voice was whispering in my ears, telling me not to go. This small but insistent voice nearly succeeded in dissuading me but the dark wings of fright beating strongly against my mind pushed me into accepting Bode's proposal.

Except through the medium of the television screen, I had never in my life seen the inside of a clinic (if we can call it that) where traditional medicine was practised. All the way down to Olotu therefore, I was trying, lamentably unsuccessfully as it turned out, to draw a mental picture of our destination. Besides that, I also wondered how Bode got to know about the "powerful man of medicine" that he was taking me to see. I had known Bode quite intimately for about fifteen years and would have sworn that his worldview was similar to mine. Now I knew better and it worried me a little. I brooded over this for some time before I put it out of my mind. After all, the man was trying to help me as best as he could.

The journey to Olotu was as uncomfortable as Bode warned me that it was going to be. We arrived dusty and thirsty but such was the urgency of our mission that we went straight to Ologbenla's compound, the home of our consultant Babalawo. In the end, we found that we needed not have hurried. The man we had come to see was not about to go anywhere. Indeed he was never going anywhere again. He was dead and we had missed his funeral by two days, no more. The fresh grave dug right in front of the compound was more eloquent testimony to this event than any number of words.

We were stunned. I could see that Bode was very much shaken by this event even more than I was. I had come to Olotu to get help and to be confronted with the grave of my would-be helper was truly unnerving. We were told that a small, black snake had bitten the man as he took the breeze close to the spot now adorned by his grave. The snake was so venomous that the great man had died almost immediately, before he could be given any help. It could be said that the end came so swiftly that in spite of his much-vaunted powers, he could do nothing to help himself. The members of his guild of Babalawos were still trying to solve the mystery of this incident on the day of our visit. According to them, there were signs that the event was, as they put it, not natural. One of them even declared in suitably grave tones that his enemies who were soon to be exposed and disgraced brought about their colleague's death.

'It is a great pity that nobody had the presence of mind to kill the snake that killed our brother' a hoary-haired practitioner declared solemnly. 'If the snake had been killed, this problem would have been solved by now because the evil-doer who, I am sure took the form of a snake to accomplish his devilish designs would also have died.'

The man saw incredulity etched on my face and shook his head sadly as if in mourning for some precious values, which had been irretrievably lost in inexplicable circumstances. He only brightened up when he noticed that Bode was drinking in his every word.

Our journey back from Olotu was very interesting to say the least. We were silent for the first ten kilometres or so, each of us locked in his ponderous thoughts. From the sideways glances, which I occasionally bestowed on my passenger, it was clearly discernible that Bode was in the grip of a very strong emotion. He had things on his mind, but he had not yet worked out how to translate those thoughts into comprehensible words and I waited uncharacteristically patiently for him to find his way out of the woods into which his thoughts had led him.

My patience was rewarded when eventually, a heavy sigh warned me that the floodgates had been opened and that I was about to be drowned in a deluge of words.

'You don't believe, do you?' asked Bode in a manner, which betrayed his exasperation.

'Believe what?' I asked in mock innocence.

'You know very well what I am talking about!' replied Bode with measurable heat.

'You know that I mean belief in the supernatural' he added after a short while.

'O oh, now I am quite sure what you are talking about, only I don't know what you mean by the supernatural. Also, the word "believe" needs to be understood in the context in which you have used it.'

'Come off it, my friend' replied Bode in a dismissive tone. 'You know very well what the word means and are only trying to be clever.'

'Me? Clever! You must be joking. If I were so clever, why am I in this fix? I am not clever and I know it, so, take it from me, I just want to be quite clear what you are talking about and that is the only reason why I want you to define the word so that we will not be talking at cross-purposes.'

I could see that Bode was not convinced by this explanation, so I went on.

'When you say "I believe that it is going to be a cold night," the meaning is quite different from when you say for example, "I believe in Immaculate Conception". The first article of belief here is based on deductive reasoning or speculation, whereas, the second statement is well, shall I say, spontaneous. It is not based on any logic or knowledge. You just know that Immaculate Conception is within the realms of possibility even though there is no shred of evidence to support your belief. For someone who does not believe in Immaculate Conception, there is no way you can convince him to see your point of view.'

'Very clever. Very clever indeed' murmured Bode, 'but I am not about to engage in semantic disputations with you, not only because it will be unprofitable, but also because I know very well that it is unnecessary. You know what I mean, so, just answer my question.'

'Well' I conceded at last. 'I know what you mean all right. It is just that I have argued with so many people on this topic that I know that what we will be throwing at each other is air, hot air.'

'There is no harm in exchanging hot air. After all, we have more than one hour to spend in this rickety car and we may as well use up the time by sending hot air back and forth.'

'Okay, I agree that we could do much worse than exchange hot air, so if we are going to talk, I want to know what you consider to be supernatural.'

'Anything that cannot be adequately explained must be taken as supernatural.'

'In that case, what you consider supernatural may in fact not be supernatural at all because what you find mysterious and totally inexplicable may in fact be quite commonplace to somebody from another environment. Today, scientists are explaining all sorts of phenomena which until recently, were classified as miracles. Take the rainbow for example. Any third year student in any decent secondary school will tell you that rainbows are formed by the refraction of light through water droplets, but there are still societies which regard rainbows as an omen of disaster and conduct elaborate sacrifices to the gods. One man's miracle is another man's science' I concluded.

Bode looked at me with undisguised pity.

'You don't know anything' my friend said after a long period of reflection. 'There are so many things happening that science can never explain and to return to your particular problem, take it from me, it cannot be resolved as long as you are in this frame of mind.'

'What has my refusal to think in terms of the supernatural got to do with my problem?' I asked with a fair degree of warmth.

'I am sure that the answer to your problem lies in the supernatural. I am not claiming much knowledge of this subject but I know enough to tell you that there are very many things, which cannot be explained now and may never be explained.'

'Can you tell me about one of such things?'

'Sure, I can' replied Bode confidently.

'Well, I am all ears' I assured him.

'There are many of these things that I can tell you but what I will tell you is related to what you have been going through. It was my uncle...'

At this point, I interrupted him, deliberately rudely.

'It is always an uncle, a friend or some such person who is conveniently absent that is always the source of stories like this. They are never first-hand experiences. Let's face it, I don't know your uncle and cannot make up my mind about the authenticity of his story. I bet if I asked your uncle about this story you are abo''t to tell me, he too will tell me that it happened to his friend.'

Bode threw me a look charged with venom. I could see that he was trying to make up his mind whether to go on with the story or not. In the end he decided to continue with it, regardless of whether I was convinced of its veracity or not. This is what he told me on that day as we rattled along in my ancient car.

'Some time ago my uncle was living in Ibadan. The room next to his in a large house in Oke-Ado was occupied by a handsome young man who was found to be very attractive by women so that he always had one woman or the other visiting him at any given time. He regarded all his affairs with these ladies as casual, so, there was a rapid turnover of girlfriends. He managed these affairs with great adroitness, but his hands were so full that there were blow-ups every now and then between girls who up till that point when they were confronted with a live rival, were sure that they were headed for wedlock with their handsome boyfriend.

'The young man was advised by several people to settle down with one of his girlfriends. He wouldn't listen. He was enjoying himself too much to give the possibility of matrimony more than a passing thought. He continued to play the field with a vengeance, at least until he was caught. He met one beautiful lady on the bus one evening and fell for her straightaway. As befitted a man with many hearts under his belt, he made a bold proposal to the lady who to his surprise and joy agreed to come and visit him at home the very next day. He could not believe his luck and was sure that he would not see the young lady again and he told her so.

' "I am very serious about my promise" he was assured. "Just tell me where you live and I will be there tomorrow evening between 8 and 9 o'clock."

' "I am almost sure that you will come", the man told her, "but, just in case you cannot come, give me your address so that I can come and see you."

'The response was a flat no.

' "You just have to believe me", the lady insisted. "I have given you my word and I intend to keep it. If you are not satisfied with that, it is just too bad because I cannot do anything more."

'The anxious loverboy had to be content with the lady's promise and came home with his head in a spin. The next day could not pass quickly enough and long before his visitor was due to arrive, he had cleaned out his room, making sure that all traces of other girls had been removed. Even as he prepared for the arrival of the visitor, he was not sure that she would come until just after 8 o'clock when she was directed to his room by one of the other tenants in the building.

'That was the beginning of an exciting period for the young man. For the first time since he came to live in that house, he was seen to be punctiliously faithful to one woman. It was clear that the couple were deeply in love with each other as the woman was a frequent visitor to the house. She however kept to his room whenever she came so that it would have been impossible for any of the occupants of the house to recognise her if they ran into her on the street, or anywhere else outside their building. The lady's mystery was deepened by the fact that not even her boyfriend had seen her in broad daylight since she always came after dark and was away long before dawn. All attempts by the poor boyfriend to find out anything about his woman failed and perhaps, out of desperation he asked her to marry him.

'To his great surprise, his proposal was firmly rejected. He had thought that his sweetheart was so sweet on him that she would only be too pleased to become his wife. He was undeterred by this setback however and continued to press his suit vigorously, until the young lady gave in and became engaged to him. The man was overjoyed and suggested that they got married immediately. His fiancée agreed with this suggestion with the proviso that he went to see her uncle in her hometown to put their case before him. The man was only too ready to comply with this request and he made immediate arrangements to go off to her ancestral home in a village just outside Ilorin.

'Only three days after this decision was taken, the young man, accompanied by my uncle went off to the village to see his prospective in-laws. They went armed with explicit directions as to how to get to her uncle's house, which they had no difficulty in finding. The old man in the rocking chair who was the first person they saw turned out to be the girl's uncle and the ardent lover, without any preamble, blurted out the subject of their mission, to wit, permission to marry his niece.

'Not unexpectedly, the old man did not give a response but bade his visitors most welcome, made them comfortable and then sent out a gang of children to summon a number of people to his presence. The children went off to deliver this message to various people who must have put aside whatever they were doing when they received the summons because they all arrived within a very short time. When they were all seated, the old man asked his guests to tell all those assembled there, the object of their mission.

'No sooner had the prospective groom stumbled over his proposal than all the women there present and even some of the men burst into tears. The visitors were astounded. What could have provoked this outburst of grief, they wondered. There was no way they could have got any answer to their unspoken query until some order had been restored and this took a long time. Eventually however, they all calmed down sufficiently for words to be exchanged once again.

' "Are you absolutely sure that you know who it is you want to marry?" the uncle asked.

' "Yes sir", was the prompt reply.

' "For how long have you known this girl you wish to marry?" asked the old man.

' "Very close to three months now" responded the puzzled young man.

' "And you are quite sure that she is the one you wish to marry?" the old man said very slowly and clearly

' "Yes sir", the young man said again.

'The visitors became even more uneasy than they already were when the uncle asked if they had a photograph of the prospective bride so that her people could verify that she was their daughter.

' "No sir, I did not think that it was necessary to bring a photograph", he said and then remembered that he did not in fact have a photograph of his girl anywhere.

' "You mean you don't have any photograph of your girlfriend. I thought that you young people are always very keen to exchange photographs."

' "That is true sir, but your daughter refused to give me any of her photographs even though I gave her several of mine."

' "And you didn't think that was strange?"

' "I did think it was strange sir, but after asking her for it several times without getting any response to my request, I stopped asking her."

'At this point the old man asked one of the younger women present to go and fetch an album from his room. The album was brought and opened at one page before it was handed over to the suitor.

' "Is that the girl you want to marry?" asked the old man, pointing to one of the photographs.

' "Yes sir", the suitor beamed, relieved that they were getting somewhere at last.

' "You are sure?" the old man insisted on knowing.

' "Yes sir, I am sure", he replied, trying very hard to disguise his irritation.

'The old man looked into all the faces around as if asking them for permission to speak, and then he announced in a flat voice, "she is dead."

'The poor suitor fainted dead away. It took quite a while before the poor man was revived and understandably, he looked dazed for a long time afterwards. He was given a hefty tot of locally distilled gin and was then told the circumstances surrounding his lover's death.

'The story was that the girl was a teacher in Ilorin and arrangements for her wedding to a young lawyer also in Ilorin had been completed. Almost three months before, she had gone to Ibadan to buy some materials, which she needed to complete her trousseau. She did not return because she was killed in an accident at a notorious bend just outside Ibadan.'

Bode finished his story on this dramatic note and waited for the comments, which he was quite sure I was going to make. But, I had nothing to say.

'Well?' he asked after a while, 'what do you think of that?'

'I don't know', I confessed at last, 'but it is rather strange that a man could make love to a dead woman for nearly three months.'

'Yes, it is certainly very strange, but let me tell you Mr Scientist, even stranger things have been known to happen.'

By this time we had got back to town and I dropped Bode off at his house and went home thinking about Bode's world which I now found was inhabited by ghosts, *Babalawos*, goblins and goodness knows what besides. I could not help but laugh at my friend's beliefs.

Two days after our trip, I bought a nice piece of roasted plantain, which I ate in my office. I thoroughly enjoyed the snack and as I ate, I looked through the piece of paper in which the plantain had been wrapped. A small news item printed in one corner of the paper caught my eye. The caption of the story was "girl dies in road accident". The story was that a girl who had just alighted from a taxi which had brought her from Orile had been run down by a bus as she tried to cross the street. The name of the girl was given as Titi and the date of the accident was the very day that Titi Ojo dropped into my life.